Thongs

THONGS

Alexander Trocchi

BLAST BOOKS
New York

Thongs by Alexander Trocchi first published in 1956.
This edition © 1994 Estate of Alexander Trocchi

ISBN: 0-922233-11-X

Blast Books gratefully acknowledges
the generous help of Donald Blaise,
Beth Escott, and Rob Warren.

Published by Blast Books, Inc.
P. O. Box 51
Cooper Station
New York, NY 10276-0051

Cover design by Beth Escott
Interior design by Laura Lindgren

Manufactured in the United States of America
First Edition 1994

10 9 8 7 6 5 4 3 2 1

Carmencita de las Lunas

On a cold morning in February 1922 some gypsies moving across country between Madrid and Escorial came upon the naked body of a woman. In this fact alone there is nothing remarkable. Spain, perhaps more than any other country in the world, is the land of passion and of death. And in Spain death is cheap, from that glittering death in the bullring to the quick thrust of the stiletto in a narrow street in a Barcelona slum. No, this death would have called for no further comment had it not been for one striking fact. The naked woman had been crucified.

Thus the gypsies saw her first from a long way off, struck like a scarecrow against the pale horizon, and as there was in that arid part of the country no crop to be protected, they approached to find out what it was.

The body was covered with thin red lacerations as though before death the woman had been whipped mercilessly with fine rods. Across the belly on a fine silver chain was slung a small metal plate which bore the inscription: Carmencita de las Lunas, *por amor.*

For love . . .

The gypsies set the cross with the corpse still nailed to it on the back of a donkey and took it to the nearest village. There they were arrested and thrown into the local jail to await judgment. The magistrate set them at liberty without hesitation when he arrived and directed that the body should be buried at once in unconsecrated ground.

This was done. And if it had not been for a chance find of mine in a Madrid bookshop three years later, the amazing story of this woman's violent and passionate life might have been buried with her bleeding corpse.

It was early spring in 1925 when I arrived in Madrid. I had gone there not only for the bullfights but also to look at the Prado, which I had not seen before. In a little street near the museum I came upon a bookshop and spent half an hour browsing amongst the old books. In a dusty pile of books in one corner, I came upon the personal notebook of Gertrude Gault, *alias* Carmencita de las Lunas. It was an old notebook with stiff covers which in one way or another had been subjected to damp; the writing was faded and in places the ink had run. I would not have given it a second glance had it not been for the fact that it was written in English.

On the flyleaf was a quotation in Spanish which I subsequently traced to St. John of the Cross. It read:

> "... *He taught me a science most delectable,*
> *I gave myself to him, reserving nothing;*
> *There I promised him to be his bride* ..."

There followed in a small neat hand perhaps the most amazing story I have ever read, a story which began in a Glasgow slum and ended in a crucifixion on an arid hillside in Spain, or rather, just before the crucifixion, for it was only upon making discreet enquiries towards the end of 1925 that I found that this woman's personal Calvary had actually taken place, and found moreover that certain influential people in Spain still made annual pilgrimages to the unconsecrated grave.

Naturally, all real names have been withheld, for it is technically, I suppose, a case of murder. On the night of the full moon in February 1922 a small group of men nailed Gertrude Gault to a wooden cross and did not leave until they had flogged her to death.

It is my considered opinion that she not only consented to but demanded this terrible act of them; that according to their own lights her executioners acted with all sense of propriety. It was her own deep sense of destiny that drove Gertrude to become Carmencita.

3
༚

To give some sense of order to the narrative it has been necessary for the present editor to return to a street battle which took place in the notorious Gorbals district in Glasgow in 1916 during the First World War. Few of the Gorbals men fought for their country. They were involved in their own bloody battles. In recreating the battle scene with which this tale begins I have had recourse not only to the notes of Gertrude Gault herself but also to eyewitness accounts collected by me between 1926 and 1930, during which years the razor still ruled the Gorbals.

It is of no small psychological interest to know that the father of Gertrude Gault was the human wolf known to all Glasgow as the Razor King and that one of her earliest adult impressions was of the mortal battle fought between this man and his own son, Johnnie, Gertrude's brother, in a Gorbals street. Who knows? Perhaps only such a brutal tribe of men could have produced a woman with such an infinite longing to be a victim.

The rest of the narrative is written almost entirely by the protagonist herself and for that reason it is truly Carmencita's book. The editorial work I dedicate with reverence to her agony.

FRANCES LENGEL

Nineteen-Sixteen

The red disc of sun seemed to be suspended at no great height above the roofs in a thin, whitish-yellow atmosphere. No heat came from it. It was more like the sun on a primitive stage set, a Chinese lantern, perfectly circular, and with no density. It was still early and the city would have been silent had it not been for an occasional milkcart, its bottles clinking in their metal-strutted boxes, some early tramcars, and the gradually increasing clamor of the church bells.

It was a Sunday morning in January and the winter-blackened trees on Glasgow Green and in the other parks in the city were gaunt and lifeless. There was as yet no sign that in a few weeks, a month at most, the sap would begin to stir in them again. In the early morning frost their trunks had the hard glint of cast iron.

With the disappearance of the January snow the city had assumed its accustomed grayness, and now under the pale yellow sky and the heatless lens of sun the streets of tenements on either side of the turgid scum-laden river were almost deserted. Their heavy emptiness, caused in part by the time of the year, the earliness of the hour, and the fact that it was the morning after the Saturday night before, was accentuated by the preponderance of gray stone, quarried locally, which went to their building. Above all other towns in the country those on the west coast of Scotland are gray, and Glasgow, the rambling metropolis of shipyards, engineering works, mining and construction companies, and endless factories, whose million inhabitants are often cut off for months on end from direct contact with the sun, is more than any other the gray city.

At the beginning there were more women than men in the group, unkempt, hatless women with bare pink legs in broken shoes, the upper part of their tired, sun-starved bodies wrapped in black or gray shawls. Occasionally, one of the women broke away from the group, shambling off down Rose Street towards the close-mouth which led to her single-end flat. But as time passed the group became larger and signs of life began to appear at the windows of the rooms which gave on to the street. The shrill coarse voice of a slum woman cried down from a window above their heads. Someone answered her. The woman at the window remained there, her flat red suspicious face craning out from the window above her flaccid breasts like some grotesque figurehead. She clutched a towel at her breasts in a thin red hand. Her mouth was open and even after she had been answered she hung there, waiting.

They were all waiting. Most of them were incredulous. But a mute hunger for violence, common to each of them, held them together, reinforcing, animating the rumor.

The men joined them, singly or in groups, coming slowly out of the closes which lined both sides of the street. The same caps, the same white scarves, the same boots. There were now over fifty people in the crowd and the excitement was growing. They were all talking at once. The woman with the flat red face yelled something to another woman who leaned out over a windowsill at the other side of the street. The other woman cocked her head, blinked, and answered with a burst of braying laughter. The crowd shifted and turned, looking up and down the street and up at the faces which looked down on them from above.

And now it was clear that the young man in the blue serge suit, a white scarf at his throat like the other men, was the main point of interest for the crowd. He was leaning with his back against the wall below a street-level window. His hands were thrust deep in his trouser pockets and he answered questions quickly and incisively as they were put to him. He looked very young, with sleek black hair and a thick powerful body which caused the too-tight blue suit to have a corrugated appearance. His face was sullen, the lips thick and sensual, and his small gray eyes were suspicious. Although the crowd made no move to interfere with him, he had the look of an animal at bay, his shoulders rounded against the wall and his heavy hands clenched in his pockets causing his trousers to bulge at the thighs. A half-smoked cigarette, unlit, hung from the corner of his mouth. He answered questions quickly but impatiently, without moving his cigarette. He seemed to be interested in those at the fringes of the crowd rather than in those close to him, or perhaps in something beyond the fringes, for as the men appeared from time to time, sidling from the closes along the street, his eyes narrowed and he watched them dangerously.

Suddenly, from a window far above his head, a metal object fell. It struck the pavement with a sharp crack and ricocheted close to his feet. A hush came over the crowd and all eyes were focused on the open razor towards which his hand after a moment's hesitation moved. He seemed to be fascinated by the broad blue blade. He tested its edge with his thumb, his head tilted to one side like a bird's, almost as though he were listening to music, and then, very slowly, almost cautiously, he closed it within its white bone handle and looked up to see who had thrown it. The crowd followed his gaze. The girl at the window on the third story pointed twice at him.

She was not pretty. Big, with thin wispy blonde hair and slack lips painted a violent red, she leaned over them all, her massive soft bosom pendulous in a blouse of white satin, and her hands clasped, her snail-white arms bent, elbows on the sill. The faces—except for Johnnie's—which looked up at her were not friendly. The men were perhaps amused but their eyes were hard and calculating. One woman shouted an insult to her and went into a guffaw. The other women joined in and soon the noise was deafening. The men joked with one another and looked up meaningfully. Only Johnnie, the young man who a moment before had been the center of attention, wasn't smiling. He had a serious, almost hypnotized look on his face, and his glance was still directed at the girl.

But she was no longer looking at him. She was cursing inaudibly at the crowd. And then, when she realized she wasn't heard, she leaned forward over the sill and spat carefully at the woman who had insulted her.

A sudden angry silence came over the crowd.

A large, big-boned man, the husband of the woman who had been spat at, let out an oath and barged his way quickly towards the close which led up to the girl's apartment. The crowd fell aside to make way for him. Johnnie watched his approach without expression. It was not until the man was within a few feet of the close that Johnnie moved. He did so with a sudden snarl, the razor flashing open in his right hand. The man stopped abruptly, a yard away, facing him. A slow hissing sound came from the crowd. Johnnie crouched, the blade ready.

"Fuck off, Beck!" he said. "Take yer bloody mug awa frae here!"

The man hesitated, glowered at the naked blade which Johnnie held rigidly at the level of his face. He stood his ground, his face white and his fists clenched at his sides. There was a deadly hush. No one moved. The faces of the spectators were twisted in anticipation.

"Ah'll gie ye five seconds tae fuck off!" Johnnie said quietly.

The long white scar which ran down the left side of Beck's face from temple to chin became as white as chalk. The young man who threatened him was speaking with his father's voice. The same voice, the same wolf's look.

Abruptly then, Beck turned on his heel and walked away. As the crowd fell back before his retreat, he said loudly for them all to hear: "Ah'm no wantin tae interfere wi the mornin's sport!"

That might have justified him had it not been for the protracted shriek of woman's laughter that rang out like the rattle of bones from overhead. Beck froze in his tracks, turned, looked over his shoulder at the young man who barred his way, and spat viciously on the street. Johnnie watched him balefully, and then, when Beck continued to walk away, he closed the razor with a snap, turned himself, and disappeared into the close.

The crowd, left to its own devices, did not disperse.

The woman was waiting for him, the door of her flat ajar. He entered cautiously.

She was standing away from the window now, near the large cavity bed, her big breasts heavy in the white satin blouse and faintly pink beneath the material. She was wearing nothing else. Her fat sluglike belly ran outwards to its own ripple and fell inwards towards her crotch with its tuft of coarse colorless hair. The color of an old man's moustache.

Her haunches were flaccid and the big round thighs were streaked gray with dirt. The legs were fat, the ankles thick, and the toenails on the spatulate toes were wedged with filth. A pot of stale yellow piss stood beside her left foot and its smell pervaded the atmosphere. An insinuation. In one of her pudgy white hands, held between two fingers stained brown from nicotine, a cigarette wilted.

She looked at him through her watery, childlike eyes, and smiled at him with slack, very red lips.

He stood watching her with a mixture of lust and loathing. She was like any one of the prostitutes in the numerous brothels in the Gorbals. But she was an amateur. They said she had money of her own.

She shuffled in her bare feet over to a cupboard and brought out a bottle of cheap spirits. She poured out two glasses. He was fascinated by the great sacklike buttocks and the thin spines of the thighs with the network of fine red veins behind the colorless sheen of hairs. Perhaps it was the imminence of death that brought his lust to a hard knot at his vitals. But excitement gained on him. He accepted the proffered glass without protest. And when she stood against him, breathing through the slack red lips at his face, he made no move to escape her.

He felt the sudden exciting chill at his loins as her hand worked loose the buttons of his trousers and a moment later he felt his sex rampant in the soft fatness of her palm.

"Come oan, Johnnie!" she said huskily.

He felt himself drawn to the bed, and with his trousers dangling below his hard buttocks his belly fitted like a blind forehead against her. He groaned as he sank into the pale lips of her sticky slit. Her hands closed over his buttocks. With an oath he worked blindly and angrily like a gouge at her heavy crotch.

It could not last long. The woman had offered herself with sure knowledge at a moment of crisis. He was back on the street in less than a quarter of an hour.

When he reached the street his face was wooden. The woman, returned to the window, looked down from her vantage point. When she saw Johnnie's gaze she made a slight movement with her hand. He was smiling when he looked down again but the smile drained away as he surveyed the crowd. It got on his own nerves as well as theirs. They were glancing at him uneasily. They were waiting.

"Hey, Allison!"

A young man of his own age stepped forward from the front ranks of the crowd.

"Go an tell the auld bastard ah'm waitin!"

Allison nodded. He turned on his heel and disappeared through the crowd.

The men nearest the front began talking now, passing the news back to the fringes. It moved quickly, like an electric spark, like a catalytic agent which caused the members of the crowd to grow together again in purpose. They were elated. All disbelief was washed out of their expressions. The women especially were watching him as he took up his position against the wall. He seemed to feel the change and respond to it. His thick features were flushed and his jacket was hanging open, disclosing the vest beneath in whose pockets at either side was a razor, the white-handled one which the girl had thrown him on the right, and a larger black-handled one on the left. They were impressed. The new item of information ran through the crowd as the first had, increasing the tension. Then as he cupped his hands in front of his mouth to light a cigarette a sudden shivering of glass on metal caused all heads to turn. A milkcart was turning into the street at the far end. He scowled as he threw away the spent match.

Slowly, a few yards at a time, the skinny white horse approached, drawing the rattling milkcart in its wake. At each close it halted while the boy mounted the stairs to deliver milk to the flats. The red-haired man at the reins sat high on the cart, slumped forward, and smoked a broken clay pipe. He was aware of the crowd which was thinning now but not dispersing. The women clustered on the close-mouths, talking excitedly, and the men, in twos and threes, leaned on the walls lining both sides of the street. They watched the snail-like progress of the cart without interest. Nevertheless, the passage of the cart along the street provided a distraction, an interval of lower tension which lasted right up to the moment when as fortuitously as it had appeared it rounded the corner of Rose Street and left the central lane of the roadway once again deserted.

At that moment, as the rear end of the cart turned the corner, Johnnie tossed his glowing cigarette butt into the gutter and closed his jacket. Three police constables had appeared suddenly where the cart had and were strolling at a leisurely pace along almost the same itinerary. The faces of the men became impassive and those who carried them opened Sunday newspapers and made the movement of relaxing against the walls. Simultaneously, those who had been hanging out of the windows disappeared from their places and the windows were closed, presenting a uniformly gray exterior. The women meanwhile gathered their shawls about them and moved deeper into the close-mouths or entered the single-end flats of their neighbors at ground level until there was no sign of a woman on the street. Johnnie, isolated now, with at least ten yards between himself and the nearest group of men, lit another cigarette, thrust his hands deep into his trouser pockets, and stared vacantly at the pavement in front of him. He remained in this posture for some seconds and then, as though the thought had just occurred to him, he extracted a neatly folded gray cap from his righthand jacket pocket and fitted it with great care close to his scalp. He looked up then, his eyes traveling along the groups of men reading their newspapers to the three helmeted constables who had stopped in the middle of the street, looking casual, as though they were discussing the weather or the architecture of the tenements, their hands clasped peacefully behind their backs in an at-ease position and their white faces under their dark blue, silverstudded helmets glancing upwards at the impenetrable windows and the sky beyond.

There were perhaps about forty men on the street, most of them ragged, disheveled, and wearing dirty white scarves at their necks, as though they had just got up and had come out for some reason—not particularly urgent—to discuss the morning's news. The church bells were still tolling and their sound on the cold windless morning seemed to be devoid of all significance. No one, certainly in Rose Street, paid any attention to them. They were there in the background, a sound monotonous and plangent in the atmosphere, and for all their movement, as flat, static, and lifeless as the red coin of sun above the level of the roofs. But there was something in the air. It was too quiet. The policemen knew it and the men, while they feigned innocence, knew that the policemen knew it, but they didn't care, for sooner or later they would have to go away, and then it would happen. By the time the policemen returned, at no matter what strength, it would be too late. It would be over.

The policemen remained in that way, a close and casual triangle, talking in the middle of the street for about five minutes, and then, as casually as they had come, they went, walking the length of the street without so much as a glance to either side, leaving Johnnie on the right unnoticed, ignored, and flicking yet another stub of cigarette where they had walked with their shining boots.

The last of them was now out of sight round the corner. Johnnie nodded to a youth on the opposite side of the pavement. The youth shambled after them as far as the corner. There he hesitated to light a cigarette, looked up and down the intersection as though to satisfy himself that there was no traffic before he crossed, and then actually did cross and held the wider-angle view on the opposite pavement. A moment later he looked back at Johnnie, nodded, and held his right thumb upwards, discreetly, at waist level. Johnnie returned his nod and opened his jacket. The razors were still there, one white and one black, the sleek silver tongues at the noncutting end of the blades pointing diagonally towards his armpits where, in the sleeve-holes of his vest, he now hooked his thumbs. At the same time he glanced down towards the other end of the street and the men, following his gaze, folded their newspapers.

Allison was approaching at a quick walk along the pavement.

The trio appeared suddenly, the father slightly in advance, and then the mistress holding the sixteen-year-old daughter by the hand. The father carried a long belt of heavy black leather in his right hand.

Johnnie saw him at once and took up his position in the center of the roadway. The crowd pressed forward and back like an ebbing tide. There was a distance of about twenty yards between the two men, the elder of whom, carrying the belt and followed at a few yards' distance by the two young women, now raised his eyes under the skip of his cap and stared drunkenly along the center lane of the street where his son, a razor in each hand, crouching ready for battle, awaited him. There was an utter silence in the street. All eyes were trained now upon Razor King who had halted, his feet apart, swaying, his powerful shoulders hunched forward like a gorilla's, and with the belt of black leather trailing the ground near his right boot. Somewhere, high above the roofs, the church bells were still tolling.

Then, suddenly, the sixteen-year-old girl had broken away from the other and was running the length of the street towards Johnnie, screaming his name. No other noise. Just the harsh strident scream of the girl and the clatter of her shoes on the stone. It took her about four seconds to reach him. And then, shifting his position slightly to meet her onrush with his left shoulder, Johnnie struck sideways with his forearm, sending her sprawling to the gutter at the feet of the nearest spectators. He was immediately on guard again, crouching, the razors held at chest level eighteen inches in front of his body. The girl was gathered into the crowd and held there by Allison and another man. In the tension of the moment as she tumbled, her skirt fluttering upwards, in the gutter, no one noticed the thin red weals which disfigured her thighs.

Razor King had not moved. His small bloodshot eyes stared out derisively beneath the lobes of his low fore-head. Now, with a peculiar shambling walk, he advanced slowly and dangerously towards his son.

He was of exactly the same stature as Johnnie, only thicker, with battle scars all over his body. His nose had been broken by a bottle flat into his face. His clothes hung in tatters from his body, but at the neck a spotless white silk scarf was wound, and his cap, like Johnnie's, was sharp and immaculate.

Now, less than ten yards apart, neither man moved. From the windows on the fourth story above the street, because of the dark clothing of the men and because of what they held in their hands—the one, razors, the other, the long black belt—the slow approach had appeared almost insectal, beetlelike. The impression was accentuated by the minute tremor in the posture of the younger man and by the slight swaying motion of the other as he advanced. When the latter came to a halt the whole street seemed to halt with him, to freeze to immobility, the crowd paralyzed by its own acute lust for violence, strung taut as a man is at the instant before he is involved utterly in love or dying, the protagonists seized in the religious certainty of their commitment, and the young woman in the yellow polo-neck jersey—the mistress—her long red hair falling to her shoulders and emphasizing the smooth rise of her breasts under the fine wool, at a dead stop, the muscles of her haunches rigid under her tight skirt and her feet in high heels riveted to the stone where she stood now, slightly to the side, nearer to the father than to the son, and unable to move.

Closer, at street level, where a light wind brushed a scrap of paper along the gutter, movement was more perceptible. The men were not still. The crouch of the younger man was not static. It increased, the tensions doubling and redoubling themselves at every fiber. And the older man, halted momentarily, had paused only so as not to provoke a sudden movement on the part of the other, but he was going forward now, an inch at a time.

His voice when it came was gruff, ominous, and strangely calm at the same time. It created the urgent necessity, as certain chords do, for resolution.

"Pit . . . doon . . . they . . . weapons!"

Johnnie didn't flinch. All things seemed to hangfire. He made no move to obey his father's order.

"Pit . . . doon . . . they . . . *weapons*, Johnnie!"

The slight note of wonder, even perhaps of hysteria, in the repeated command seemed to draw the crowd actively into the situation. It participated in nightmare.

The voice which shrilled out now was irrelevant, absurd. It was Allison's. His face craned whitely forward from behind the daughter whom he held, her back towards him, close to his chest.

"Ye bloody well asked for it, Gault!"

Razor King's face became contorted with fury. The black belt shook in his fist. He glared hatefully behind his son in the direction of the voice.

"Aye, Allison! Ah've got ye marked!" he bellowed. "This is your fuckin work and ye'll pay for it! Ah'll come roon tae yewze in jist aboot two meenutes!" He looked at Johnnie again, his face set and his bloodshot eyes narrowed to slits.

"Ah'm tellin ye for the last time, Johnnie! Pit . . . doon . . . they . . . bliddy . . . razors!"

At that moment, and for the first time, Johnnie wavered. His muscles seemed to slacken. A low moan escaped the crowd. Razor King breathed outwards through his twisted nostrils. His chin was tilted slightly to one side, giving the head a cocked appearance.

It might have been over.

But the next voice, a harsh slum-woman's scream, acted as the detonator.

"Ayee! Awa' back hame an get yer bliddy erse skelpit! It's no that long ago yer mither wiped it fur ye!"

Johnnie moved then, straight for his father.

With a thin animal snarl Razor King hurled the belt from him. His hands flashed for his vest pockets and the gleaming blades cut forward at his son's rush. Johnnie ducked, too late to avoid having his left cheek slashed open to the bone, but quick enough to be under his father's guard and to butt him with all his power with a knee to the groin. Razor King screamed with rage and pain and toppled backwards, bent like a hinge. Johnnie hesitated for a split second, and then, with the wild cry of a wounded animal, leapt cutting and kicking forward. More like a ghoul than a man he went in, his cheek streaming dark red blood, his mouth bellowing inarticulate words, and his terrible razors cutting. Razor King went down under the onslaught, powerless to protect himself. And Johnnie had no mercy. His newly tacketed boots began systematically to break the bones of his father's body. At that moment he was insane.

Somewhere in the near distance a police whistle blew, a thin clear sound in the cold morning air. That was the signal for the rammy to begin.

Somebody at the edge of the crowd leapt in with a broken bottle. It was Beck. He was on to Johnnie before the latter knew he was confronted by another assailant and the beer bottle struck jaggedly into his head above the left ear. He collapsed at once, the razors tumbling from his clenched fists.

The crowd, excited by the continuous blasts of the police whistles, became a riot. Women fled screaming to the close-mouths. Men, uncertain whether to flee or to attack, were struck down from behind and trampled underfoot. No man wanted to be a victim. Razors, bicycle chains, and broken glass appeared electrically in their hands. A moment later Rose Street was involved in one of the most venomous brawls that ever took place in the Gorbals.

The police made a truncheon charge as soon as they arrived, sixty of them, thirty from either end of the street, forming an impenetrable blue cordon. They struck brutally in two waves and the crowd caved in, those who could escaping into the closes.

Fifteen men, including Johnnie, were carried by stretcher to the infirmary, thirty-two—amongst whom were four women—by police van to the central police station, and Razor King alone was carried by horse-drawn ambulance to the morgue.

Gertrude

The first time I saw her was when he pushed her in front of him and told her to strip. Just like that. She was frightened. You could see she had been half-unwilling to come. She glanced over to where I was lying in the cot. It seemed to take her by surprise, that I was there I mean. And that made her hesitate. My father was half-drunk as he always was in those days.

"Get yer bliddy clothes off!"

She looked as though she wanted to get out. She was unsure of him. Although afterwards she told me she wanted it too. Like we all want it, hard, like a pain. I could see her body was quivering. That set me on edge. It was infectious. To see flesh shudder like that. You wanted to touch it. That night was the beginning of something new for me. I envied her. I couldn't take my eyes away.

"In front of her?"

She was looking at me.

"You go tae sleep," my father said to me. But I could see he didn't care. She did. At first anyway. Not after. I thought at that time she was innocent. I didn't know.

I pretended to close my eyes.

"Now get yer bliddy clothes off!"

She didn't hesitate long. She slipped out of her canary-yellow pullover. She always wore that. It suited her. It had a roll neck. The straps of her brassiere were dirty. It was made of white satin and was taut and pearly over her full breasts. There was sweat on her belly just below her rib cage, and under her armpits where the hair was black, and wet like a soft paintbrush, not red like her hair.

Then she removed her skirt. She had big thighs, smooth and big. And they looked slightly hot and sooty near the crotch where the satin was, and that looked greasy as satin does from sweat. Hazel's cunt sweated a lot. I could see that.

My father was watching her. He had lit a cigarette. He was still wearing his cap which he wore low over his eyes, like a visor. He was looking at her feet first, the high heels, and then at the smooth stocking-clad legs, and then higher up at the white expanse of thighs, ballooned and soft under the elastics from her garter belt. She had nice flesh.

My father made a kissing sound with his lips. And then he laughed.

She was embarrassed.

"Take aff yer bosom-bag!" he said with a sneer.

Her nipples were big, not quite red. More like the color of an old dental plate. They were the firmest breasts I had ever seen. You wanted to lick them. I could see why my father wanted her. He could see she was hot.

He was still smoking, the cigarette held between his lips, and the smoke rising in a steady wisp in front of his small screwed-up eyes. I watched fascinated as his right hand unbuttoned his fly.

His thick white cock sprang out like a living thing and grew between his fingers into a shining poppy. He played with it gently, looking at her, a conductor with his baton. I could see he was smiling as it rose and fell like a pointer in his hand.

My own naked body had become numb and heavy under the blanket. It was as though I discovered my hand at my crotch. I didn't remember moving it there. My fingers were already sticky with the sap that flowed from my cunt.

I was nearly fifteen at that time. The boys were already beginning to look at me. And the old man who repaired boots in Cumberland Street had waggled his penis just as my father was doing now. He went through the glass door which led to his back shop and if a girl was alone he would take it out and tap the glass with it. You would be standing waiting and suddenly notice it, like a big finger beckoning you. The last time I had been there I nearly went. I wanted it and I didn't. I think he knew that. But I didn't want to have a baby. I left the shop without the boots.

The way my father moved his cock reminded me of the bootmaker. There was something sly about it. Ingratiating and threatening at the same time. A big smelly finger. You wanted to put your nose to it. At that moment I felt jealous of Hazel. She was excited. And she was going to get it. Like a fist. My own body already felt it.

"Rub yersel'!"

My father's lips were drawn back over the yellow stumps of his teeth in a kind of snarl.

Slowly, hesitantly, Hazel lowered her right hand to her mound. Her fingers slipped into her delicate cleft. Her body shuddered. In her high heels she seemed a little unsteady, like a fine racehorse on icy cobbles. Her body quivered under the motion of her fingers and her long red hair splashed down over her firm breasts. Through hair her green eyes stared at him almost defiantly.

He let his hands fall to his sides and tossed his belly so that his cock swung up and down as though on a spring. He grunted each time he did so. He was trying to make her hate him. To make her hotter.

Her nostrils were quivering. She looked beautiful. I envied her.

He shuffled towards her, his knees close together, until he was almost touching her bare flesh, and then his right hand shot out viciously and pushed her backwards towards the cavity bed. For my father fucking was rape. He was a wolf and he liked nice fat fear-ridden bitches for his lust. White thighs.

It was a high bed built in an alcove. It was broad and shadowy. It must have stood nearly three feet from the floor. As she fell backwards her naked buttocks slapped against the wooden side. He held her there in a firm grip. She was wilting. He was muttering obscenities at her while his hard calloused hand worked roughly between her soft legs until her head drooped like a bell of burnished copper on his shoulder. His prick was hard and flat against her naked belly now, and his hands slipped round behind her to support her smooth buttocks. He lifted her quivering torso high so that she toppled backwards, all legs, the thighs apart like broken calipers. I could hear her panting. From where I lay I could see only her legs now, all the power gone out of them, dangling like white creepers over the side of the bed. The rest of her, her soft front, arms and head, was out of sight on the cavity bed.

Razor King walked over then and switched out the light. At the same time he locked the door.

He seemed to be unaware of me. In the darkness I thought frantically of the old shoemaker behind the glass, trying to see him. If it had been then I would have gone like a sleepwalker.

Behind closed eyelids I heard Hazel groan as though she had been wounded for a long time. The bed shook. I shuddered.

Somewhere above there was the sound of a clothes' pulley going up on its iron wheels and a woman's laughter, like the sound of a night animal beyond the damp walls. The atmosphere of the room seemed suddenly to be impregnated with the smell of young woman and male. The grunting grew furious. And the slap of wild bellies. I pulled the blanket over my head and passed the flat of my hand downwards slowly over my own throbbing front. Someday soon, I felt, it would happen.

25

ॐ

ॐ

The next morning, Sunday, I was awakened by the sound of church bells. People were already moving about in the rooms and passages of the tenement. Night changed to day gradually, for the tenements were never silent. The inhabitants were born, they made love, and they died, in the same rooms, and often at night. Just before dawn, and before the sounds of the milkcarts in the street outside, there was probably more silence than at other times, an hour's silence before the paraffin lamps went on in the fetid rooms. And all night long doors slammed and people shuffled about, moving for whatever purpose to the common latrine on the stairs.

My father was snoring heavily in a drunken sleep. His new mistress lay with the upper part of her body exposed and with one slim white foot sticking out of the covers at the bottom of the bed. I had the impression that she was not sleeping. I knew why.

When Hazel allowed my father to bring her home she made what many regarded as the most important decision of her life. And there was no going back. From the moment that he took her on the cavity bed she was a marked woman. She belonged to him, like his bloody razors.

Razor King, the werewolf of the Gorbals.

More like an animal than a man he emerged from our one-room flat in the tenement and before he had reached the street the word of his approach had traveled a block. Men retreated behind doors or crossed to the opposite pavement; women appeared at the close-mouths smiling, showing off their ragged figures.

John Gault seldom looked at them. If he did, he looked at them with a pure male look, his gaze traveling from their haunches to their bunched breasts and then up to the flushed face on which fearful consent was already written. Sometimes he would pause and shamelessly run his hand up between a woman's thighs under her skirt. If the woman pleased him he would go with her to her room. If not, he would burst into loud laughter, thrust his finger into her cruelly and hurl her whimpering aside.

No woman was ashamed to go with Razor King. It was a mark of caste. A girl took on an air from being a victim of his lust.

But he had brought Hazel home. And that was different. My father would mark her, a small cross cut with a razor on the soft inner surface of her left thigh; his cattle brand.

Hazel told me afterwards that she was slightly drunk when he picked her up. She was on her way back from a dance hall with another girl when Razor King barged out of a pub on to the pavement in front of them. The other girl screamed, not loudly, and he stood glaring at them with his red-rimmed eyes. His glance soon left the other girl and fixed itself on Hazel. She said that when he smiled it was as though she already felt his hands on her naked flesh. She was weak at the knees. He beckoned her to him. She hesitated. A little crowd had formed nearby. Men stood in the pub door. The organ-grinder had stopped playing. She flashed a look at the men and then back at Razor King. A young man stepped between her and him. He didn't have time to say whatever it was he was going to say. A moment later he was stumbling backwards into the gutter, his ruined mouth hanging on his throat and a small gusher of blood squirting high above his shocked face. Razor King beckoned to her again, this time with the bloody razor. She said it was as though she had lost all power of will. She went up to him like a lamb. Without a word he took her arm and walked her past the crowd along the street, leaving his victim bleeding, perhaps to death, in the gutter.

When she realized where he was taking her she had been afraid. Everyone knew about the mark. Fourteen women in the Gorbals had been cut already. Normally my father kept the women for about two months afterwards. Then they were free to go. The men of the Gorbals fought each other to marry a marked woman. It showed deference to the King. It was sure protection.

But she was frightened all the same. Up till that time she had avoided him. Hazel never wanted to stay in the Gorbals. I didn't learn until later that she had other protectors and that they were not averse to her receiving the mark of Razor King.

Hazel said she hadn't slept. After he had fucked her she had lain awake for the rest of the night thinking about the mark. She couldn't sleep. And her head ached from too much drinking. She couldn't believe it was her in bed with him, she said. And she was thinking that tomorrow her father would know and she was wondering what he would do. Time had never passed more slowly. When dawn came, the gray light filtering across the room, across the basin of stagnant washing water on the table, she was in a cold sweat and her shoulder ached with the weight of my father's head.

Johnnie hadn't come in. Hazel didn't know that and Razor King hadn't noticed but I had because Johnnie had mentioned her name a week before. He said he had big eyes for her. A real hot piece of stuff. He might even marry her. And I was wondering how he would take it when he came in and saw her in bed with our father. She couldn't have been more than a year older than Johnnie, who was seventeen. Johnnie would be mad. I knew that.

I got up and walked quietly over to the cavity bed. I was right. Hazel was awake. She looked at me without saying anything. She didn't know me then. I was his daughter, that was all she knew.

My father was snoring heavily. Hazel was trying to cover her breasts. It was as though she was ashamed to let me see them. I noticed that she had been bitten in a number of places by the bugs. Here and there on the smooth alabaster skin of her upper torso was an ugly red spot. It was almost impossible to keep the bedbugs at bay in the old Gorbals tenements. We used paraffin for everything, for light, and the men used it for hair oil, and we used it to fight the bugs with. We smeared it on the walls.

I smiled at her, trying to tell her not to be afraid. She didn't smile back. She was too scared. Her lovely round breasts rose and fell next to the rough gray blanket. I would have liked to touch them but instead I turned away and began the day's work.

I raked out the fire and lit a new one, took the basin out to the stairhead lavatory and emptied it, and then I sat down on the pan to pee. There was a used condom, its neck tied with a knot, near my right foot. I slipped my foot out of my shoe and touched the little rubber sack with my bare toes. I was cold but it made me feel sexy being as I was with my naked bottom on the wooden seat. I wondered who'd been in the lavatory the night before. It was used often for that. Greta Smith told me she'd let a boy do it to her there. Against the wall where the dirty drawings were. They made me feel sexy too. Sometimes I masturbated there, looking at them. When I lifted up the condom I found it was quite heavy.

29

It was a bit sticky and the dust had collected on it. I wrapped it up in a bit of newspaper and put it in the pocket of my skirt. The thought of its being there, the real stuff, so close near my cunt, made me feel really good. I was going to begin rubbing myself when I heard footsteps on the stairs. I knew at once it was Johnnie. I called out to him.

"That you, Sis?"

"Aye, just a minute, Johnnie. Ah'm comin out."

He was waiting for me. He had a smirk on his face and looked pleased with himself.

"Where were you all night?" I said.

"That'd be tellin!" he said with a wink.

I knew all right where he'd been. He'd stayed the night in a brothel with a whore. Otherwise he wouldn't have been so pleased with himself. He was earning money now with a coal lorry.

"Is faither angry?"

I told him then about Hazel.

"Faither didn't notice ye wis nie there."

Johnnie had gone white.

"So he's taken Hazel Cooper has he? Ah'll get the auld bastard fer that yet!" he said between his teeth.

When I had finished tidying the room I put a kettle on to boil and went out to buy milk and the Sunday morning papers. I left Johnnie huddled over the fire, staring at it.

When we had gone in together Johnnie had taken one look at Hazel, who was still lying beside my father with her naked breasts exposed. Then, without a word, he had turned his back and sat down by the fire.

I went out and downstairs.

There were no men in the street. The men of the district usually had a long lie on Sunday mornings. But the women were already moving about, in and out of the dairy and the news agent's.

Old Mrs. MacBride caught me as I came out with the milk from the dairy. She wanted to know if it was true my father had taken Hazel Cooper. She said she had heard talk. Someone had told her that Henry Cooper, Hazel's father, who worked as a night watchman in a warehouse, had been looking for a gun. He said he was going to blow out John Gault's bloody brains.

"Aye, there's them before that tried!" I replied, and once again, for it wasn't the first time, I felt proud at having Gault for a father.

But I was worried about Johnnie so I evaded the others who tried to talk to me and hurried back to the single end.

Johnnie hadn't moved.

I lifted the boiling kettle off the hob.

At that moment Razor King woke up. He shook his head with a grunt and ran his fingers through his close-cropped hair. Hazel, nervous, and as if to appease him, leaned across him and kissed him softly on the lips.

He blinked at her angrily.

"Lay aff of it, ye sexy little sewer!" he snarled. "Fur Christ's sake has that bliddy erse o'yours no had enough of it!"

She cowered away from him into the dark corner of the alcove. He didn't pay any further attention to her. He sat at the edge of the bed, naked from the waist downwards. His feet were filthy and the skin of his legs under the thick growth of blue-black hairs was gray. At that moment he caught sight of the two bottles of beer Johnnie had brought home with him. He lurched off the bed, screwed off the top of one of the bottles, and drank a deep draught. The liquid spilled around his mouth and ran down over the beating vein of his neck on to his dirty undershirt which he seldom took off. Before he drank again he wiped his mouth with the back of his hand and rubbed away the trickle at his chest. He drank again, this time emptying the bottle. The alcohol had an immediate effect upon him. His humor changed. He screwed the top off the second bottle, took one or two small gulps from it and turned to Hazel, offering it to her. She watched him like a rabbit watches a snake. She shook her head. He shrugged his shoulders and walked on his hard-soled feet to the sink where, drinking again, he began to urinate. He allowed the tap to run for a moment afterwards. Still at the sink and gazing out of the grimy window, he drank the rest of the beer. He put down the bottle, turned on the tap again, blew his nose into the sink, and sluiced his face with cold water. He came away rubbing his face with a towel.

As he stepped into his trousers he asked me if breakfast was ready.

I said it would be in a minute and dropped two slices of bacon into the frying pan. They began to sizzle immediately.

At that moment Razor King caught sight of Johnnie.

He looked at him suspiciously. Johnnie still stared into the fire.

"Whit's wrang wi you?"

"The King's up. No peace noo," Johnnie said laconically.

"You mind yer bliddy lip or ah'll show ye who's King!"

"Aw fer Christ's sake can ye no leave a man alane!" Johnnie stood up.

"There's only one man in this hoose," Razor King said with a laugh, and then, pleased with himself, he added: "How d'ye like the tert, Johnnie?" He nodded towards Hazel, who was now sitting up with the blankets pulled up to her chin.

Johnnie turned and looked at Hazel for the first time. His expression became disdainful.

"Is she no a bit skinny?" he said.

"Skinny?" the King said. "Show him ye're no skinny, hen!"

Hazel didn't move.

Razor King strode across to her, whipped off the bedclothes, and scooped Hazel out of bed. She tumbled on the floor.

"Get up," he said.

Slowly, one stocking still trailing round her ankle, Hazel got up. She was stark naked. Her pubic hairs looked damp. They curled in little black wisps.

"Ah thought her hair wis red?" Johnnie said. But he was looking at her in a different way. He was fighting to control himself.

"Aye, she's a wee smasher!" my father said, pride of possession in his voice.

Hazel turned away angrily. She was beginning to notice that she had been bitten by bugs during the night.

She climbed on to the bed and began to examine her spots one by one.

Johnnie was fascinated by her. He couldn't keep his eyes off her now. Her movements were soft. Her flesh had quivered enticingly as she had climbed on to the bed. The skin of her buttocks was smooth, like the surface of mercury.

"Ye got yer eye filt?" Razor King said to Johnnie with a sneer.

"Aw, shut yer fuckin mouth!" Johnnie said turning on him.

For a moment it looked as though my father was about to strike him, but Razor King's anger left him almost at once. He decided to take it as a compliment. He laughed again and said he could understand Johnnie's jealousy. Then he walked over to the bed and with two fingers began to play with Hazel's cunt. She stiffened and shot a glance over Razor King's shoulder at Johnnie. Razor King was making the sound one makes to a cat, teasing her pubic hairs.

A moment later, with obvious effort, Johnnie turned on his heel and went out. As the door closed my father bellowed with laughter, slapped Hazel playfully on the belly, and turned to me and asked for his breakfast.

"This is Gertie," he said.

୫୬

"Gertie'll stay."

Breakfast was over.

My father was sharpening one of his razors on a

leather strop. Hazel, with my coat across her shoulders, was smoking a cigarette and trying to appear calm. But I knew she wasn't. I knew she couldn't be.

I asked her if she wanted another cup of tea to give her time, but she said she didn't.

"Clear the table," my father said.

I did so. At the same time I brought the iodine and the bandage. It was a ritual. I had officiated before. Seven women I had seen spread-eagled naked on this table, the operating table. And always the same smell. The female sweat. For they all sweated as they first sat and then lay back across the hard wood. Some more than others. It stood out like little needle points on their muddy white skin. Almost an execution. And the faint smell of rum. My father always gave them a swig of rum before he began. I remembered the last woman, Sadie Bell. A big-arsed woman with big breasts. She couldn't control herself. Even before the first cut she began to piss. Razor King beat her up for that. She had welts all over her when she lay down again in her own mess to be cut. I was hoping nothing like that would happen with Hazel. I wondered what I would do myself if I had been in her place. But I knew I never would be. Only Razor King marked his women. No one else would have dared.

Hazel had put on lipstick. There was a dark red smear on the end of her cigarette. Her mouth was sullen and yet relaxed. Her almond-shaped green eyes—greener because of the striking redness of her hair—expressed nothing.

Did she know? Was it possible she hadn't heard? I didn't think so. Everyone knew, everyone in the Gorbals anyway, that no woman came to Razor King's house without receiving his mark. It was an unwritten law. I had often heard women discussing it. And sometimes in a dimly lit close a group of girls would get together with a lipstick and play at "marking," a little vermilion cross on the left thigh, three inches from the cunt. I had painted one on myself often although I was perhaps the only girl in the Gorbals who could never carry the authentic one.

Razor King was pouring some rum into a glass. He poured it liberally, about the size of two doubles.

He carried it across to her.

She looked up at him questioningly.

"Drink that," he said. His voice was almost gentle.

She accepted it meekly and drank.

"Take yer time, hen," he said. "We've all day."

She nodded.

"When ye're ready," he said, "just lie doon across the table. On yer back."

At that moment Johnnie came in again. He took in the situation with a glance. He knew what was going on.

"Branding day," he said sarcastically.

"Get awa oot o'here!" Razor King said.

Johnnie ignored his father.

"Yer faither's doonstairs," he said to Hazel.

Hazel's eyes flashed.

Razor King glanced at her and then back at Johnnie.

"Get awa doon an tell him to go on hame!"

"He won't listen to me," Johnnie said.

I could see Johnnie was enjoying himself. He was looking derisively at Hazel, who pulled my coat tighter around her naked body.

"Hey there, John Gault! Come on doon here tae the street like a man!"

The voice came from the street, two stories below.

Razor King swore.

"It's auld Cooper. Her faither," Johnnie said with a grin.

Razor King reached for his cap.

"Wait, Razor King!"

Hazel ran over to the window and opened it.

"Away hame, faither! A came here o ma own free will! Away on hame!"

"Ye bliddy wee whore!" the voice came back. "If ye're no doon here in two meenutes ah'm comin up fer ye!"

"Ah'll kill the auld bastard!" Razor King snarled, but before he reached the door Hazel had thrown herself naked on to his arm.

"It's no him ye'll mark, Razor King!"

She was trembling, the slick white slats of her flesh pressed against his raggedly clothed body.

Johnnie had stepped into the room and was standing beside the fire warming his hands.

Razor King put one arm round the panting woman and lifted her bodily into his arms. He carried her across to the table.

"Lock the door, Gertie," he said to me. "An' you see that no one comes in here!" he said to Johnnie, who nodded, pretending to be uninterested.

Hazel was breathing heavily. She was spread-eagled like a starfish on top of the wooden table, the lower part of her legs which were bent at the knees hanging down over its edge. With each hand she grasped one edge of the table as though to brace herself against shock. The back of her neck fitted at the fourth edge. In that position the middle part of her young and ripe torso, radiating in every muscle and hair a living shudder, was bared to her executioner. I returned from the door and stood over her, looking down. Gently I placed my hand on her lean belly just above the strong and hairy torque of her mound. She smelled of sweat like the others. It was at the armpits, at the navel, under my hand, and at the warm pit between her trembling thighs. I wondered what she was feeling. She had closed her eyes. In my other hand I held a piece of cotton soaked in iodine, ready to swab the wound. With his left hand my father gripped her just above the left knee. Like a strong clamp. And then, his eyes narrowed, and still wearing his cap which he hadn't bothered to remove he leaned down, with his face over her thigh and with his right hand touched the blade of the gleaming razor to the taut skin. It broke apart almost magically in a thin red line. Hazel's torso shuddered under my hand. I laid my left forearm across her chest just above her coral-tipped breasts to prevent her from rising. She appeared to derive comfort from this movement. She exhaled her breath, her nostrils quivering, and seemed in spite of the pain she must have felt to give herself over entirely to the cutting razor.

My father worked swiftly, cutting two minute triangles of flesh from the thigh. The blood was flowing like a small tide when he finally wiped his razor on his sleeve.

Hazel uttered a sharp gasp of pain as I applied the iodine-soaked cotton to the wound. The tears were running down her face. As I bandaged her thigh I heard Johnnie laughing. Razor King was looking at him. Dumb. Like a wolf. But Johnnie laughed. He went on laughing.

※

Night fell early in the Glasgow slum. At half-past four in the afternoon I lit the oil-lamp and sat down with the *News of the World* in front of the fire.

The rest of the day had passed uneventfully. Old Cooper, still hurling threats at our window, had finally been led away by some of the men. But he was not to get off so lightly. Razor King never forgot an insult. One night a few weeks later old Cooper was badly slashed by an unknown razor slasher on his way to work. Everyone knew it was my father's work but as usual there were no witnesses and the victim kept silent. Cooper lost his job and half-blind and emaciated he took to selling bootlaces in the street. I speak of this simply to emphasize the fact that it never paid to cross Razor King. The latter's position depended entirely on his reputation for the most savage brutalities. Thus sooner or later a man who had crossed him would find himself confronted in a quiet place by a man half-mad, more wolf than man, razors flashing and hobnailed boots kicking. Cooper was just one of a long series of broken victims. His fate excited pity in no one, not even, I believe, in Hazel who, having been brought up in the slums with a knowledge of all its brutal conventions, looked upon her father as an old fool, just as she would have considered it foolish for a man to

※

try to stop an avalanche with his fists. Anyway, since she had come to bear Razor King's mark she had become his woman, and as her fate was intimately bound up with the fate of her man her first loyalty was naturally to him.

Hazel had returned to bed immediately after the marking. She was sleeping restlessly. Johnnie and Razor King had gone out. I was therefore alone. Remembering suddenly, I put the paper aside and reached in my pocket for the little screw of newspaper. It was still there, warm from the warmth of my body. I opened it and threw the paper in the fire. I held up the little yellow rubber sack to the lamp and watched the liquid move about like crystalline sputum within. I tightened the knot at the neck to make sure that none of it escaped. Then I poured some hot water into a basin and washed the bag carefully. Clean and dry, it lay like a little sexual talisman in the palm of my hand. I laid my other hand on top of it and crushed it between them. The fluid moved about excitingly between the palms. I shuddered, aware that my own breathing had become heavier. I laid it against my cheek. All skin with the slimy little clot within it was more than anything else like an oyster, a warm yellow oyster, a gift from an unknown man. Had it been inside a woman, a man's lust trapped within the almost transparent rubber in the hot breathing walls of some unknown woman's cunt? I shuddered with pleasure at the thought. What a wonderful find! I had seen them before, often, in closes, dunnies where we went to smoke cigarettes, and lying around the street; but I had never before found one which was so skillfully knotted so that not a drop of the precious ichor was lost. I raised it to my nose and smelled it.

I was slightly disappointed. It smelled only of rubber. I had washed the living smells away with the dust. I held it by the knot and allowed the bag to fall like an empty sausage skin on my lap. I lifted it again and watched the slime fall like a veil within to the little nipple at the end of the condom. Imprisoning the liquid there between my forefinger and thumb I raised it to my mouth and sucked it strongly as I would have sucked a teat. That made me feel really sexy. A man's lust in my mouth. I pricked the rubber gently with my teeth, little doting pressures, little tongue jabs, ecstatically. With a furtive glance at the bed where Hazel still slept soundly I allowed my knees to fall open and allowed the fire to strike hotly at my naked crotch. I raised my skirt above my navel and looked down at myself. There was a small mole below and to the left of my navel, a little mark which would soon be covered by my growing pubic hairs, which were as yet still sparse, quite silky and not extensive. The lips of my sex showed pinkly through the meager hairs, wet or sticky like the pistil of flowers. Slowly, allowing the bag to wing between my reddening thighs—the wave of heat from the fire struck directly—I touched it lightly against the sensitive clitoris. I was breathing heavily. But somehow this slight contact disappointed me. Once again forcing the fluid into the little bulb at the end I held it tightly to my sex and rubbed it there briskly until the exterior of the condom was again quite wet. Then, with my middle finger, I slipped it into myself up to the knot. Only the open end of the little rubber bag was now visible. I closed my legs tightly together to contain what was in and with my eyes tightly closed I enjoyed the sensation.

At that moment Hazel groaned.

Quickly I allowed my skirt to drop back into place and got up. I found that I could move around without hindrance and all the time with the luxurious feeling of having that between my legs.

"What time is it?" Hazel said. She was in a sitting position and now seemed wide awake.

"Nearly five," I said.

"Will ye make us a cup o'tea, hen?"

The big kettle was already near the boil on the hob. I moved it over until it sat directly on the fire. It began to sing at once. I was smiling to myself. I was wondering what Hazel would say if she knew what I had between my legs. It suddenly occurred to me that my father never used condoms. For all she knew, Hazel might be pregnant. I would like to have asked her what it was like to be fucked like she was the night before. Did she really want it in the same way as my father did or did she only want the reputation? She was already well-known in the dance halls. That's where Johnnie had seen her, dancing with one of the professionals, for she had a reputation as a dancer herself. I had been a bit surprised when she came back with Razor King. There would be no more dancing for her now. Not until my father got tired of her anyway and by that time she would probably be pregnant. And that would be the end of her. She would settle down with some man or other in a slum flat. She would become one of the hairy, one of the gaunt, hatless women in shawls. My mother was one of those women. I suppose everyone thought I was going to be one too.

I made the tea and carried a cup over to her.

She was looking at me in an uncertain way, as though she wasn't sure whether she could talk to me.

"What age are you, Gertie?

"Fifteen," I said. "What about you?

"Eighteen," she said. "Eighteen last August."

"Were ye no thinkin of gettin married?"

"Me marry!" She burst out laughing. "When ah get married it'll no be tae one o'the louts in this district! No bliddy fear! Ah suppose ye think ah'll marry a hooligan like your brother Johnnie?"

"Whit's wrang wi'im?" I said angrily.

"Whit's wrang wi'im!" she mimicked. "He's all cock an bluster, your Johnnie! No brains!"

"An ah suppose Razor King's the same!" I said.

She laughed softly. Her breasts were above the blanket. She took her right nipple between her middle and forefinger and squeezed gently. "No. He's different," she said. "He's the King. That's different."

"Johnnie's only seventeen."

"Who cares if he's seventy!" Hazel said. "He's no the King and no likely tae be."

"Ah widnie be too sure aboot that!" I said and went angrily over to the fireplace.

For a moment we were both silent.

Then Hazel's voice came softly across to me, coaxing.

"Ah don't want tae quarrel with ye, hen. When ye're a bit older and know a bit more aboot it ah'll tell ye a few secrets."

My hand brushed my skirt above where the condom was embedded.

"What do ye mean?"

She laughed again.

"Ah'm no that young," I said.

She looked at me reflectively.

"Step a minute into ma shoes," she said, pointing to the patent leather high-heeled shoes which lay discarded beside the bed.

I was thrilled. I had never worn high heels. Slowly, with great excitement, I crossed the room and put on the shoes. They were not much too big for me. I stood up shyly for her to see.

"Lift your skirt a bit above your knees and let's see ye," she said. "Now turn round."

I was careful not to lift the skirt too high. I didn't want her to see the projecting condom.

She seemed pleased with me.

"Ye're no half bad, hen," she said. "Razor King's daughter, eh?"

"Whit difference does that make?" I felt it was an attack on me.

"It makes a difference all right. Don't you worry!"

When I didn't reply, she said: "Ye can thank yer bliddy stars!" Her tone became confidential. "Listen, Gertie," she said, "ye don't want tae stay in the Gorbals all yer life, do ye?"

I shook my head. We all hoped that some miracle would happen, that some Prince Charming would come along and take us away. But it never happened. Deep down we all knew we were condemned. Did Hazel know a way out? Then why was she with Razor King? I looked at her mistrustfully.

"Come here an ah'll show ye something, hen."

I went slowly up to the bed.

"Now this is between you an me," Hazel said. "You breathe a word tae yer faither or that precious brither o yours an we're finished. Ye can rot where ye belong, right here in the Gorbals."

I nodded breathlessly.

She opened her handbag and from out of the lining she took a small rectangular book.

"D'ye know whit that is?"

I shook my head.

"It's a bank book," Hazel said. "It tells how much money ah've got in the bank." She opened it. "Look there," she said. Her finger pointed. The deposits amounted to two hundred and fifty-three pounds.

❧

That night I couldn't sleep. For a long time I lay listening to the grunting animal movements of Razor King as he made drunken love to Hazel. I lay in the darkness with the nipple of the condom in my mouth. Johnnie hadn't come in. I knew he wouldn't come back that night. When I felt they were asleep I slipped quietly out of bed, dressed quickly, and let myself out of the flat. On the stairs I hesitated. Where was I going at this time of night? It must have been after eleven. The streets would be deserted at this time of night. But something dragged me on. I couldn't sleep. My whole body cried out to be taken. Hesitantly I descended the gaslit stairs past the stairhead lavatory on the floor below. Although it seemed deathly quiet I sensed that there was someone inside. I waited long enough to hear a man whisper and a woman answer softly, urgently. Then I went on down into the close. I walked quickly through it to the street. Without paying much attention to where I was going I walked along towards the first intersection. It was cold and everything was very dark. I walked quickly. Somewhere ahead of me I saw a man wearing a cap move into a lane. He moved furtively, as though he was afraid. I walked quietly until I came to it. Flats above formed a tunnel over the entrance to the lane. Beyond the tunnel, in the open, a single gaslight bracketed to the brick wall burned. I could see no movement. Nervously I entered the tunnel. I was scared and yet I was throbbing deep between my legs. And then, as I moved hesitantly out of the other side of the tunnel, I ran into him. He was round just out of sight from the street in such a position that the gaslight illumined him for himself only, and for me, for I was within a yard of him. He looked up startled at my approach, and then his gaze fell downwards to what was in his hands.

His cock was long and stiff, like a mast, the foreskin pulled well back over the glans penis. All of it was out, the testicles as well. He had pulled them through the slit in his underpants. He said nothing. He looked from me down to his rampant cock and then back to me again, and when I said nothing but stood there gazing first at him and then down at his glistening cock a slight leer appeared on his face. Still without a word, but leaning towards me almost confidentially, he took the thick pink member near its root and made it quiver between his fingers. It grew even bigger and seemed to be beckoning to me obscenely. He was smiling now, first at me and then at his cock. He turned towards me. I could smell his breath. He had been drinking. Slowly I reached forward and took it in my fingers. He quivered at my touch. And then suddenly I felt myself grasped at the scruff of the neck and pulled close to him. He was laughing softly.

He had forced me against the wall so that we were both out of sight from the road.

"Kneel down!" he whispered urgently.

I found myself kneeling in front of him with my bare knees on the cold cobbles of the lane. His cock was dancing against my face. It smelled unwashed, of sweat. He gripped my hair in both hands and forced my face against it.

"Get it in, ye fuckin slut!"

With one hand he guided it against my lips and moving his belly forwards rammed it in.

I almost choked. His hard nob was rammed right into my rising gorge. I closed my eyes and gave way to his will, making my mouth a soft receiving hole for his lust. All resistance was gone from me and when he sensed that his hands tightened on the hairs of my head more cruelly and a stream of obscenities came from his mouth. In the midst of my delirium the knowledge came to me that I was in fact suffering pain. His violent movements caused my knees to be scraped on the stones. My scalp was afire under his clawing fingers. My throat was almost in convulsion. And yet there I was eagerly lending myself to this brutal treatment. That was perhaps the first realization of the destiny that was in store for me.

Who this man was I never knew. Suddenly I felt the spurting hot semen in my mouth. I sucked avidly, draining him to the dregs. Suddenly I felt myself hurled away from him. His open hand struck me painfully on the side of the face. The force of the blow sent me sprawling on the ground. I heard his heavy breathing and his curses. I was lying face downwards in the middle of the lane, my fists clenched, my eyes tightly closed, my whole torso quivering with pain and pleasure. A moment later I felt my skirt being ripped away at the back and the cold night struck my naked buttocks. I groaned with pleasure, uncertain of what was to come. And suddenly a red hot poker seemed to be laid across my thighs. I found myself screaming and even in the middle of the scream I realized that the pleasure was there, like a healing blanket over all pain. Through the mists of hot sensation I heard the noise of his fleeing boots and I realized that my scream had scared him. When finally I pulled myself to my feet, painful all over but with a slow electric current of joy burning within me, I found myself alone in the cold dark lane. I shuddered, seized suddenly by shame. What kind of love was this of which I had been the willing victim? What strange desires lurked in the breast of a fifteen-year-old girl? Razor King's daughter? Did my blood mark me even more terribly than the sweating women who were victims of his bed?

My skirt was torn. I wrapped my coat tightly about me and walked as quickly as I could back towards the tenement. As I climbed the stairs I heard a woman's groan issue from the privy on the landing. But it bore no resemblance to my scream in the lane. It was a soft groan, husky, as though a man had set his member between her thighs.

M<small>Y</small> father was waiting for me. The lights were on. He was sitting at the table with a whiskey bottle in front of him. He had obviously been drinking heavily. Hazel was reading a comic, sitting up in bed. My father looked up at me with dull red eyes as I came in.

"Where the bliddy hell hae you been!" he said quietly and menacingly.

I was shaking with fright. I knew I couldn't take off my coat without him seeing that my skirt was torn away at the back. And just before I entered I had touched my fingers to the weal across my buttocks. I suppose he used a belt. It would be red and livid.

My father was looking me up and down, at my shoes, at my bleeding knees, at my face.

"Ye filthy little whore!" he snarled. "D'ye no think ah know where ye've been!" He poured himself another glass of whiskey.

"Take yer bliddy coat off!" he said.

There was nothing else for it. I did so, trembling. At once his eyes alighted on my naked thighs.

"Turn round!" he said. And when he saw the weal: "Ohoo! So he stropped yer erse fer ye too, did he?"

In the background I was aware of Hazel watching me speculatively.

"Who was it ye filthy bitch!"

I cowered away from him. "I don't know!" I said desperately. It was the truth. I hadn't recognized the man.

"So ye don't know! Well ye'll know who gives it tae ye noo!"

He got up and lurched over to the nail on the door where his black leather belt hung. I watched him in fearful fascination. If he had gone for the belt a week ago—both Johnnie and I had been belted regularly since were were little children—I would have experienced nothing but fear. But the whole situation that night had the acute color of sex. As he reached up for the thonged leather I experienced a vivid thrill of anticipation. It held my fear at bay, as something which hung threateningly outside me.

"Get yer clothes off!"

I obeyed at once. There flashed through my mind the memory of Hazel's position the evening before. She had been forced to strip in front of me. She had a strange smile on her face now. I stepped out of my torn skirt and slipped off my pullover. I stood naked in front of him.

That made him hesitate. He stood staring at me uncertainly. My breasts had grown over the last year. I was nearly a woman.

I moved before him. I lifted myself face downwards over the wooden table. The wood was cold against my naked belly and breasts. I felt my flesh quiver with excitement at the thought that here on the wood Hazel was going to be witness to my humiliation.

Perhaps it was my willingness to be thrashed that made his first strokes light. They stung but were almost purely pleasant. I gasped each time the leather belt fell. My legs had slipped apart at the crotch. Suddenly he stopped and I heard him say: "What the bliddy hell's that!" I felt his fingers between my thighs and then I had the sensation of having something ripped out of me. Only then I realized. It was the condom! I had forgotten all about it.

"Jesus Christ!" I heard him yell. "Ye bring his bliddy dirt back wi'ye! Stuck between yer stinkin little legs was it!"

I knew then that I was going to be thrashed without mercy. Hazel let out a gasp. And then the belt fell like cinders on my naked buttocks. I screamed. But it came again. The pain seemed to spread like a sea over my whole shuddering torso. I screamed again, barely conscious of the mumbled reactions of the neighbors beyond the walls. Even yet there was no tear on my cheeks. I felt I was going to explode. The belt came again and again, and each time the tears welled up in my eyes, they were sucked down again by some invisible whirlpool of lust within me. And then the tension cracked. I screamed with all my might and the tears of my body out of control flowed out in great sobs. Only then did I realize that Razor King had stopped. The door slammed. Somewhere beyond me my pain came back, a long shuddering wail, and it was my own lips slobbering on the wood.

A moment later I was lifted gently off the table and helped over to my cot. Something burning was forced between my lips. I had the swimming vision of Hazel holding a glass there and I realized it was whiskey. I swallowed, and then, my body reacting mechanically to all the cruelty of the last hour, I vomited until I could vomit no more. I lay quivering on the camp bed. Hazel was running her fingers through my hair. That night she said only one word to me, softly, and repeated it over and over again. Her head was between my thighs and her tongue darting smoothly against my clitoris. "Come!" she was saying. "Come . . . come . . . come . . . "

৯৫

I was in bed off and on for a week. Johnnie asked me more than once who it was who had interfered with me. I said I didn't know. Finally he lost interest. Razor King ignored me. Only Hazel seemed to take an interest in me. She had drawn closer to me. She had become like an older sister. She got the whole story out of me, how I had gone after the man into the lane and how I had knelt before him and sucked him fervently. I also told her about the condom.

"You liked being belted, didn't you, hen?" she said one night when we were sitting alone by the fire.

I was taken aback. How had she guessed my guilty secret? My words came haltingly. I did and I didn't. It had been terribly painful. But deep down I had a hunger for it, an obscene animal hunger that filled my body like a nausea.

"It's nothing to be ashamed of, hen," Hazel whispered. "Some women like it. They get their pleasure that way."

Was that possible?

Hazel put her hand on my thigh and squeezed it.

"I've a date on Thursday night in the West End," she said. "I'll take you with me if you like."

"Will you! Oh, please, Hazel!"

"I said I would, didn't I? But mind you behave, and don't breathe a word to your faither or that brother o'yours."

I promised.

Hazel still referred to Johnnie as "that brother o'yours." It was not until nearly two years later that she became his mistress. And a great deal happened in that two years.

The following Thursday Razor King was off on one of his periodic bouts of drunkenness. He would spend all his time for many days in the pubs and in the brothels. Johnnie too was out of the way with a gang of the younger men who were planning a raid on a dance hall in the Plantation district.

We left the house at seven. That morning Hazel had gone out and bought me some new clothes, a sleek black skirt with a cut up one side, a red polo-neck pullover, and some frilly underwear. Just before we left she handed me a pair of sheer black nylons. As soon as we were out of the Gorbals, Hazel called a taxi. I was thrilled. I had never been in a taxi in my life before. She gave an address somewhere in the West End and we sat back comfortably. She said we were going to have a good time, that I needn't worry about that. I was already having a good time. I had never looked so pretty and I was smoking a cigarette openly. "Just you do as I tell ye, hen, and everything'll be fine," Hazel said.

We drove up a quiet avenue. The houses, each in its own grounds, were hardly visible from the street. For some reason or other Hazel stopped the taxi, paid off the driver, and we went the last hundred yards on foot. We turned in at a massive gate hung upon stone columns covered with climbing ivy. She pulled the chain of the bell. "It wouldn't be safe to drive right up here," she said. "We've got to be careful. There's too many busybodies in this world." I didn't know what she meant, but I didn't care. I had every confidence in her. To think she knew the people who lived in this mansion!

A man in a butler's uniform approached us down the short drive. He bowed politely to Hazel as he ushered us in. In the large hall he took our coats. In the rear, a wide marble staircase led up to the floors above. Even the hall was richly furnished with parquet flooring and vividly colored rugs. We were shown into one of the rooms at the side.

A serious young man with spectacles came into the room at once. He was dressed in a black suit with drainpipe trousers. He wore a frilled white shirt with a large flopping violet cravat. He went at once to Hazel and kissed her hand.

"Mr. Oakes is not here yet," he said apologetically. "He was detained in the city. We might have a drink until he comes. I believe he is bringing some friends with him."

Hazel nodded as if she knew what he was talking about. I was looking round the room. It was almost empty except for half a dozen armchairs and the silky black rug in front of the massive open fire. The walls were covered with some kind of red satin fabric in which here and there was a filament of gold thread. They were entirely bare except for one large painting which hung in the center at one end. It looked like a crucifixion. When I examined it later I was amazed to find that a woman was nailed to the cross in place of Christ and that every detail of superbly rounded torso, the heavy mass of the crotch, the navel, the breasts, even the hairs under the armpits, had been painted minutely in. But from where I stood at that moment I couldn't make out the detail, and the arc light which was placed on the floor underneath it was not switched on.

"This is Gertrude Gault," Hazel said, interrupting my reverie. And then, to my horror, she added: "She's Razor King's daughter."

"His daughter!"

The young man whose name turned out to be Harry Prentice came up to me at once and kissed my hand. I must have looked startled for as his head came up his eyes looked into mine, curious and penetrating behind his thick spectacles.

"I have heard a great deal about your father, Miss Gault," he said, "but I'm sorry to say I've never seen him in action."

I was even more surprised. Could it possibly be that there was nothing to be ashamed of?

"Well, well!" the young man was saying, "his mistress and his daughter on one night! Mr. Oakes will certainly be pleased."

Hazel stood with her tightly-clad young haunches turned to the fire. I thought she was really beautiful.

"And now, what will you drink?" Harry Prentice said.

"Gin and lime for me," Hazel said.

I didn't know what to say.

"She'll take the same," Hazel said.

Harry seemed to pull a cocktail cabinet out of the wall. A few moments later we were all seated near the fire with the drinks in our hand. After a while Harry Prentice noticed that my attention was drawn to the painting at the end of the room. He said at once: "Just a moment and I'll switch on the light." He did so by pressing a button under the mantlepiece. I got up hesitantly and walked slowly across the room towards the picture. It was as I approached that I suddenly realized it was a woman. Close up, I was able to see the beautiful radiance of her expression. She seemed to be dying and smiling at the same time. At that time I didn't know that the face was like one painted by Botticelli. The light from below had the effect of making her seem to bend backwards like a bow on the cross to which her hands and feet were nailed. The entire body, the proud breasts, the subtle mold of belly, the flat thighs, was scored with narrow red weals. As I stared at it uneasily a shaft of doubt moved silently within me. What did this mean? And why did I feel so intimately involved with the beautiful victim on the unholy cross? I felt myself blushing.

And then a new voice, the voice of an older man who must have entered the room while I stared at the picture, boomed out beside me: "Well, my dear? What do you think of her?"

Almost without thinking I replied at once: "She's beautiful!"

And then I turned to face them.

The older man was not alone. Three other men dressed in dark jackets and gray striped trousers stood expectantly near the door. They were all tall men of between forty and sixty.

The man who had spoken, Mr. Oakes, was also tall and slim. He had an ageless face with penetrating eyes.

His well-kept hair and moustache were flecked handsomely with gray. He reminded me of a British Prime Minister and I realized at once that I was in the presence of a man at least as impressive.

He laughed lightly at my answer and turned to his friends. "Come in, gentlemen! Harry will get you something to drink." He turned back to me. "I believe your name is Gertrude, my dear, and that your father is the . . . er, Razor King! I want you to know how delighted I am to have you as a guest tonight! My name is Charles Oakes. I am a good friend of your friend, Hazel."

I glanced across at the fireplace where Hazel still stood smoking a cigarette in a long black holder. I wondered again about her. How did she ever get to know these men?

"Thank you, sir," I said.

A fleeting expression of displeasure passed across Mr. Oakes's distinguished features. But it passed quickly.

"Come, my dear," he said gently, "I wish to introduce you to these other gentlemen." We returned near the fire. "Mr. Bing, Mr. Duval, and Mr. Coldstream. Miss Gertrude Gault."

The gentlemen bowed.

We ate in another room, much larger than the first reception room. The long wooden table was candlelit and although the table itself was bright enough I found it difficult to make out the rest of the furniture and decorations. Mr. Oakes sat at one end of the long table and I was surprised that I was given the place at the other end, opposite him. Mr. Bing, Hazel, and Mr. Duval sat on Mr. Oakes's right, and Mr. Coldstream and Harry Prentice on his left.

It was a copious meal with many courses served professionally by two footmen. But I had no appetite. I was too excited. Over and over again I asked myself what it was all about. Why was I here? Why was Mr. Oakes interested in me?

"You're not eating, my dear!" Mr. Oakes called gently from time to time from his end of the table. I blushed and replied that I wasn't hungry.

Mr. Oakes made some remark that I didn't understand, something about spiritual hunger, to Mr. Coldstream, a blond man with a red and slightly beefy face. Mr. Coldstream laughed in a funny way: "Ha, ha . . . ha, ha . . . ha, ha!" and twinkled at me from his side of the table. I blushed.

From time to time one of the footmen filled one of the many wine glasses in front of me, but unlike the others I hardly touched the wine.

After the last course, before coffee, Harry Prentice got up, nodded to Hazel who got up also, and they both left the room. I made as if to follow but Mr. Oakes beckoned me to remain seated by raising his finger.

"We shall join your friend later," he said reassuringly.

Coffee was served, and a few moments later, brandy in huge brandy glasses.

The men talked amongst themselves. They seemed at first to be oblivious of me. After a while I became conscious that my end of the table was brighter than the other. When I looked up I noticed that a soft light was being shed upon me from the ceiling. This gave me quite a start. I darted a look along the table at Mr. Oakes. It was then that I realized they were all looking at me.

"Don't be frightened, Gertrude," Mr. Oakes said, calling me by name for the first time. "We are about to ask you some questions. I want you to answer them truthfully. If you tell any lies you won't be invited here again. We shall know. These gentlemen and myself have a way of knowing."

I felt afraid, even more afraid than I was when I was taken to the headmaster's office at school. That was for writing something on the wall of the girls' lavatory in the playground.

"What age are you?" Mr. Oakes said.

"I was fifteen yesterday."

"She's very young," Mr. Bing said.

"That is excellent!" said Mr. Duval.

"Have you ever had anything to do with a boy or a man?" Mr. Coldstream said.

Before I could answer Mr. Oakes held up his hand.

"One moment please, gentlemen! I think we should impress upon Gertrude that we are already in possession of the true answers to all the questions we pose. A childish indiscretion could ruin everything. I have great hopes for Gertrude. We should be careful."

"I entirely agree," Mr. Bing said.

Mr. Duval and Mr. Coldstream nodded.

"Listen carefully, Gertrude," Mr. Oakes said. "A short while ago you left your father's flat one night. Your father had just made love to Hazel and they had fallen asleep. You went out alone into the street. It was very late. You were driven by a great sexual need. You saw a man turn out of the street into a dark lane. You followed. The man had begun to masturbate under a lamp when you arrived. Of your own free will you got down on your knees and took his sex in your mouth. Later the man struck you with a belt. When you returned home your father held you naked on the table while he flogged you. You took pleasure from everything that happened. We know all this already. That is why you have been invited here tonight."

I realized at once that Hazel had betrayed me. I hated her! Now everyone knew my secret shame!

"What did you feel when you took the big prick in your mouth?"

"Did you swallow his semen?"

"Did he touch your cunt?"

"Do you often masturbate?"

"What would you like to do most?"

"Would you like to be whipped with leather thongs?"

"Has a man ever put his prick into you?"

"What do you feel when you hear your father making love to Hazel?"

"Did you enjoy it when Hazel made you come with her tongue?"

"You feel guilty, don't you?"

"You feel you ought to be whipped, don't you?"

"And you would enjoy that more than anything, wouldn't you?"

"What do you do to yourself in the lavatory?"

"You carried a used condom in your cunt for a while, didn't you?"

"You're feeling sexy even now, aren't you?"

The questions were thrown at me in rapid succession. I was in tears as I answered. Yes, yes, no, yes, yes, no, yes!

YES! YES! YES! I answered frantically but I did not tell a lie.

Half an hour later my interrogators seemed satisfied.

"She is a virgin," Mr. Coldstream said at last.

"Our Virgin, I hope," Mr. Oakes said seriously.

The others agreed heartily.

"And now, Gertrude, we shall join the others," Mr. Oakes said.

All the men stood up. I did likewise. Mr. Oakes took me gently by the arm and he led the way down a flight of stairs to a cellar corridor in the basement. At the end of the corridor we passed through a double doorway into a large, brightly lit room. The floor was covered with straw and the walls and ceiling were thickly padded with a kind of canvas quilting. On the far wall hung a painting identical to the one in the first reception room. But there the resemblance of the two rooms ended. This room was filled with big wooden blocks scooped out in places to fit the shape of the human body, with leather thongs and belts, and innumerable chains.

Hazel stood beside Harry Prentice near a large wooden board which was held firmly at the perpendicular by wire guy ropes. It was about six feet broad and seven feet high with thongs of leather hanging from it at various levels. A hole, about nine inches in diameter, was cut in the heavy wood at a level of about three feet off the ground. I heard the double doors close softly behind us. I looked at Hazel.

She was entirely naked except for a diminutive skirt of knotted leather thongs, about the thickness of the laces of football boots, which lay loosely round her hips and failed to cover the hairy mound of her sex. She also wore sandals of thonged leather and metal-studded leather cuffs at the wrists. Her whole body was made up to accentuate the voluptuous curves and her eyes had been treated with mascara to look twice their normal size. In her right hand and falling down against her right leg she held a vicious-looking cat-o'-nine-tails.

Harry Prentice was also naked except for a leather belt heavily studded with iron which he wore round his waist. He, too, wore sandals. On his head was a black skullcap which fell into a shaped mask over his eyes. He was already rampant, his big prick standing stiff like a ship's boom at his middle. Instead of leather cuffs he wore gauntlets. He carried what looked like a fat candle from which a thousand fine wire tails, about eighteen inches in length, sprouted softly.

"Excellent!" said Mr. Oakes, who still held me gently by the arm. "We have been longer than we expected and there isn't a great deal of time. Mr. Bing and myself have to be off to London tonight."

"We are ready, Mr. Oakes," Harry Prentice said.

"Good." He turned to Mr. Coldstream. "Will you go first, Coldstream?"

Coldstream nodded without speaking.

"And you take your clothes off, my dear," Mr. Oakes said to me.

A terrible panic seized me. Hazel noticed it and came quickly to my side. "Don't you worry," she said. "You won't get anything you don't want." She began to help me off with my clothes. The cat-o'-nine-tails dangled from a loop on her wrist as she did so.

Coldstream was already naked. He too had a massive hard-on. He was breathing heavily, his red face even redder. When he walked over to the board and stood with his front flat against it, the holes on a level with his lower belly and his rampant member protruding at the other side of it, I was shocked to see the state of his back and buttocks. New redder scars were laid across the old pinker ones. From the back of his knees to his neck his body was a mass of lacerations. It was then that I noticed the holes for the feet at the base of the board. His feet passed through them and his ankles were bound tightly with leather thongs. His arms were stretched sideways and upwards and similarly bound.

I, too, was now naked. Harry gripped me by the upper arm and led me to the other side of the board. I had just time to see Hazel take up her position behind Coldstream with the poised cat-o'-nine-tails.

In front of me now was the circular hole filled with Coldstream's white front with its chevron of fair hairs, from the navel to the tops of the thighs, and jutting forward the swaying cock and the tight pink pack of his testicles.

Suddenly I heard the first swoosh of the cat. I heard Coldstream groan. The cock quivered. Harry threw me down on the straw and gave me a light whack on the buttocks with his wire scourge. It didn't hurt. It tingled pleasantly, tantalizingly. "Go on, take it!" his voice said gently.

I crept on my knees closer to the quivering penis and held it in my hands. It gave me an indescribable thrill. The cat swooshed again, and Coldstream's voice cracked out like a pistol shot: "Suck it!" Harry gave me a harder swipe on the bare buttocks to encourage me. I moved forward at once, taking the shining nob in my mouth and cupping, compressing the testicles in my hands.

The cat struck more quickly now with hardly a pause between the strokes. I had no need to move. With its own ecstatic shudders Coldstream's cock was accomplishing itself in my mouth. As his white lust streamed forth he screamed with pleasure and pain. I sucked him avidly to his roots. I heard the cat swoosh three times more before Mr. Oakes's calm voice directed Hazel to stop.

"Your turn, Duval," Mr. Oakes said.

A moment later Coldstream was helped down and a new front was thrust hard against the board. This time it was bristling with shaggy coppery hairs, the balls enormous, and the cock short and thick like the body of a fish. Warming to my work, I ran the tip of my pink tongue amongst the hairs of his lower belly as he was tied in place, and then, with the first swoosh, I forced the thick member between my lips and sucked deep. Duval screamed from the beginning. The shuddering motion soon caused the semen to leap hot from his pipe into my gullet. I felt a light stroke of the scourge on my back and I crooned over the throbbing penis as though I were sucking a teat.

Next came Mr. Bing, pony-colored and slithering quick to loose his hot slime. Mr. Oakes's pink cock in its nest of black hairs came at me next, dancing like a serpent in my slime-softened mouth. After he came I sank back on my young and trembling haunches, exhausted and lathered in sweat.

I felt myself being lifted gently under the armpits. It was Harry again. "Your turn now," he whispered softly in my ear, and as he spoke I knew that I wanted it. My cunt was throbbing with excitement. Invisible chains seemed to hang from my thighs and desire made my soft belly bounce against the wood. The thongs were secure. I felt a tongue thrust at my clitoris. Whose tongue I don't know. Everyone seemed to be on the other side of the board. Except Harry who was evidently to be my executioner. Executioner! The word slips easily from my pen, like an omen!

"Use the scourge, Harry," Mr. Oakes said. "Not too much violence."

And then it began. My buttocks were struck by the thousand fine wires. If you can think of a shatter of glass, in the skin, in the sensitive layer of flesh beneath, or of a cracking of pores—it was not one redhot lash of fire, but a general cracking ache which caused my front to sweat and shudder against the board. At the third stroke I screamed. A needle of delight passed through my clitoris and I had the sensation of being balanced there, my body swinging on the fulcrum of my sex, in an agonizing ecstasy. Once again the tears refused to rise. A flask of boiling water on a flame, a tube sunk in it, and the water rising and falling within it, just failing to reach the top. Again the bursting sensation, of lungs and heart—ayeee! And the tears came like a flood, and then there was nothing but ache and the terrible relief that it was over.

Strong hands helped me down. Brandy was forced between my lips. Then I was carried into a pleasant room where for two hours I slept.

When I awoke Hazel was bending over me.

"Are you all right, Gertie?"

I smiled in reply.

"Let me help you get dressed," she said softly.

Half an hour later the long black Daimler left us at the edge of the Gorbals. We walked quickly back to the flat.

❧

Six months passed. Each time I asked Hazel when she would take me again she was evasive.

"You mustn't be impatient, hen. You're young. You have plenty of time . . . "

Plenty of time! Oh yes, plenty of time! But what of the present? What of the agonies of starvation my body suffered during those months? Had I failed somehow? Had they decided against me?

I fell back into the old life of the slums. My body was maturing quickly. The young men of the district were beginning to be very interested in me. One had even suggested that he would like to marry me. How sorely tempted I was! Would a young and virile husband not bring relief to my starved body? But then I thought of the children and the squalor. To move from this single end to another identical, what was the point? Hazel said I had fifty pounds. She had shown me a bank book in my name but she said that I couldn't touch it, that she was keeping it for me. Surely, if they had given me all that money, they must have liked me! I didn't know what to do.

Only one thing provided me with distraction at that time. Johnnie was approaching his eighteenth birthday and as the weeks passed his muscles grew harder. Razor

King still fucked Hazel and made no move to change her for a new mistress but he spent more time getting drunk and in the brothels. I knew even then that it was only a question of time. One day Johnnie would challenge our father's authority.

More and more Johnnie stayed in the house when Razor King was out. As the days passed he troubled less and less to conceal his desire, and at times, especially when Hazel was scantily clad and washing herself in the tin basin, he would sit astride one of the chairs a few feet away from her, his elbows resting on the back, and an expression of ironic amusement on his face. He seldom said anything. He just sat and watched.

Johnnie was probably the only man in the Gorbals who would have dared lay a hand on Razor King's woman. He dared, when finally he did so, because he was the same man his father was, only younger, and with the absolute knowledge of the young he sensed his own growing manhood and compared it to the man who was dying in his father. He had little love for Razor King. Our mother had been one of Razor King's women and both Johnnie and myself had seen her on more than one occasion before her death struck bleeding on the floor, our father, the black belt in his hand, swaying drunkenly above her.

On the other hand, Johnnie didn't blame Razor King for this. The poison of hatred was to a great extent neutralized by an intuitive sympathy of one rogue male for another. Such incidents between husbands and wives went on all the time in the Gorbals. Men like Johnnie and Razor King were untroubled by conventional notions of justice. Things happened. Blood was spilt. A man reacted to the immediate situation. And if he had the reputation of being a wolf he had to live up to that reputation. If you have terrorized all men over a period of time you become the slave of your own brutalities. Any deviation, any mercy shown, is interpreted as a weakening. And a weak wolf doesn't become a dog. A weak wolf is destroyed.

In a way, Johnnie admired our father. Simultaneously, he despised him for a dying man. There had been many Becks, men not quite brave enough to deal with the wolfish John Gault, and who had been marked for life because of a wrong word, but Gault was growing old, drinking too much, spending too much time in orgies with whores, and Johnnie knew that there would be other men, younger, unwasted, braver, more cunning men, and one day Razor King would be battered down on a stone pavement.

Johnnie was waiting. He had nothing to lose.

On the street he was recognized as the son of Razor King, a young man who was fast growing to be his father. Few men would have dared to cross him for fear of his father's reprisals. It was as though he had decided to wait until his father suffered the defeat that was bound to come. His position depended on courage and strength. He didn't lack courage and never would, but the strength was gone. One day he would die or be beaten as some boxers are into idiocy.

Johnnie knew this, and Hazel knew it, and so did I. Johnnie waited, enjoying in a detached way, a spectator. I watched with excitement. It was all I had during those long months I wasn't called to the big house. I had no love for our father. Only his brutality fascinated me. And if that brutality could be smashed by another's I would be fascinated no longer. I watched Hazel. She didn't resent Johnnie's ironic attentions. Sometimes, I felt she encouraged them. I knew that one day she would give herself to him and that then it would be a matter of days.

But all this was not enough.

I was starved. My father had not laid a finger on me since the night he thrashed me naked on the table. And my body cried out for brutal treatment. Once tasted, the sweet poison of punishment is irreplaceable. What could an ordinary man offer? Caresses? A sentimental love?

It might have been eight months after my visit to Mr. Oakes's house that I realized I could stand it no longer. It would have been easy to give myself to one of the boys in the communal privy on the stairs, but he would want sex, the ordinary lustful sex with his naked belly on mine and his seed eventually in my womb. Any one of a hundred would have been glad to serve me, even to marry me, especially perhaps to marry me, for I was every bit as beautiful as Hazel and I was the daughter of Razor King. Intuitively I knew that whoever I gave myself to would try hard to get me pregnant. And that did not fit in at all with my plans. I suspected that Mr. Oakes required me to be a virgin. I might allow myself any sexual extravagance short of the ordinary act of copulation.

I left the house one day about two o'clock in the afternoon and it was not until I was nearly there that I realized where I was going. Cumberland Street! To the shop of the lascivious old shoemaker!

Of course! Why hadn't I thought of it? He would be glad to give me what my body demanded. My cunt began to itch as I walked quickly towards his shop.

As I turned into Cumberland Street he was opening the door for the afternoon's business. I stopped abruptly and stared at him. He looked up and saw me. Something in my expression must have told him I had come to see *him*. He was between fifty and sixty with a bald head and a gray bristle on his face. He had a slight stoop. When I made no move to walk on, a small smile played on his thin lips. His hand fell down to his crotch and he gripped the meat there beneath his dirty brown corduroys. He held it speculatively, looking at me, his lips apart, his tongue licking the upper one. And then, when I still didn't move, he darted into his shop out of sight.

I followed him like a zombie.

The interior of the shop smelled musty, of leather. He was nowhere to be seen. But I knew where to look for him. He was in his usual place, in the back shop, and he had his bare cock out and was tapping it like a soft fat pencil against the glass. When I walked straight to the connecting door he jumped aside in glee and, stuffing his penis back into his trousers, opened the door for me.

When I went in, he put his fingers on his lips like a conspirator and said: "Shh!" Then he darted out to the front shop and locked the front door. He pulled down the blue blind. And a moment later he came back through, his old stubbly lips trembling.

"Ah've seen you before?"

I nodded.

He thrust his hand at once under my skirt and stuck his middle finger in my cunt. I leaned against him, breathing heavily. Over his shoulder I saw bundles of leather bootlaces on his workbench. He forced me against a wall and thrust his small potato mouth against mine. His tongue slobbered against mine. I made no effort to resist. It was important that I should capture him completely.

He was very nervous. I wondered if I was the first who had actually entered his lair.

When finally his mouth came away from mine I put my lips against his ear and whispered: "I want to be whipped!"

He pushed me away to arms length and stared at me greedily.

"You'll take all your clothes off?"

I nodded passionately.

His false teeth clicked. He reminded me of a dirty sheep. He was shivering with anticipation.

"On the couch," he said.

He pointed to a dusty old horse-hair sofa at one side. It was at that moment piled high with shoes.

"Won't take a minute," he said breathlessly.

While he stacked the shoes on the floor I stripped naked. My body was covered with a cold sweat and my flesh was quivering.

He turned to face me. When he saw I was naked he let out a small excited croak. He threw himself on his knees in front of my cunt and started to lick me furiously. I let him do it, working my hot and sweaty crotch against his stubbly mouth. I groaned with pleasure. He lapped the slime out of me like a thirsty dog. I came, shuddering, with his old bald head jammed like a hot turnip between my thighs. He felt me come and lapped furiously. Then, a little exhausted from having stood while he did it, I slipped away from him and lay face downwards on the horse-hair couch. My flesh quivered at its cold rough touch. I rubbed my cunt there and my smooth white buttocks quivered.

"The thongs!" I whispered huskily.

He nodded quickly. But first he stepped out of his trousers and threw his dirty underpants aside. His old cock stood out bent like a boomerang and twitching.

"The thongs!" I whispered urgently again.

He took a handful of leather bootlaces.

"Take one first," I said huskily. "On my buttocks, as hard as you can!"

He obeyed. The thin leather thong cut my buttocks.

"Again!"

He struck again.

"Again!"

He struck for a third time.

I was quivering with pleasure.

"Now take a handful and strike me all over, on my thighs and my back as well!"

He thrashed me soundly. I came twice under the punishment. I asked him if he had a thick belt. He was shuddering with emotion and I noted a bead of sperm at the end of his prick. He, too, had come in punishing me. He produced a black leather belt, not unlike my father's. "Thrash me with that, as hard as you can, ten times!" I begged him.

His eyes glinted.

"Be my master!" I breathed passionately.

That set him erect again. A cunning look came on his face.

"You'll do as I say!" he said.

"Yes! Oh, yes!"

He cut me hard with the leather belt. I writhed in agony. All the time he muttered filthy obscenities at me.

"Give me your cunt again!" he commanded.

I turned over and raised my cunt to his face. He sucked away all the accumulated sweat and slime. I thought he would never get enough. Then, suddenly, he was going to shove his prick in me.

"No! Not that! *I* want it!"

He grinned delightedly and brought it near my face. I took it at once between my lips and sucked all the sperm out of his old body. Then I turned on my face and lay exhausted. A moment later I felt his face on my buttocks and his tongue, like a soft scoop, was working at my anus. I strained and brought a soft turd into his slobbering mouth. Then we both slept.

It was dark when we woke.

He lit a paraffin lamp and stood staring down at me. I noticed that his cock was erect again and that he was masturbating. When I went to take it in my mouth he shook his head. He seemed to derive pleasure from my watching him. He grunted, winking at me all the time. Then, when he was about to come, he threw himself voraciously on my arse and I felt his big prick burst painfully into my tender anus. The pain was excruciating, but gradually the familiar sensation of pleasure overriding pain came to me. I twitched beneath him like a landed fish.

Who would have thought there was so much pleasure to be derived from one old man?

I stayed with the shoemaker until ten o'clock at night. Just before I left he hooked his finger in my cunt again and drew me close.

"Next time it'll be better!" he croaked.

He knew I would come back.

ॐ

It was a full year before I saw Mr. Oakes again. I knew that Hazel saw him at least once a month and as her fair body was never lacerated I presumed she fulfilled the function of whip-mistress solely. Sometimes I was able to look at her bankbook when she was at the lavatory and I saw the steady increase in her savings. It was about that time, just before my second meeting with Mr. Oakes, that I began to feel superior to Hazel. She was simply a paid professional. For me, on the contrary, the realm of pain and pleasure was a religion. It was unthinkable that I could ever earn my living in the way Hazel did.

After I met my shoemaker I no longer looked forward with the same desperation to the day when I would be invited to visit the big house again. Old Willie knew that my young body was demanding, that the more terribly he inflicted humiliations and punishments upon me, the more urgently my body and soul cried out for their increase. And he was an accomplished leather smith. In a short while he had created not only the most fiendish of thongs with which to lacerate my trembling flesh but had also fixed pulleys to the ceiling and floor of his back shop, so that my young torso, thonged at wrists and ankles, could be stretched and held taut like a quivering bowstring of flesh, and in four or five excruciating positions, to meet its punishment. He became a master in the art of flagellation, the high priest of my terrible cosmos of pain. He did everything with adoration, thrashing my flesh, thrusting his old lips voraciously into my sweating cunt, twisting thin black thongs of leather around my thighs with a stick. He made many instruments. Perhaps the most terrible of all was the simple leather instrument which he called "The Prick." It was a long cock of laminated leather as thick as and three times as long as a strong man's rampant member. Had he not used it with great care it would have been a killing instrument. It could be used either as an instrument of flagellation or as a ravisher. Other interesting implements were "The Brush," "The Beads," "The Balls," "The Crushing Cunt," and "The Five-Fingered Spranger." The last was a masterpiece of simplicity and efficiency: five eighteen-inch rods of flexible steel covered with leather thrusting from a handle shaped like a human hand.

Perhaps I would be spread-eagled like a spiderweb between floor and ceiling while he was licking my cunt. I asked him what he intended to do to me.

He would give a small throaty laugh.

"A good brushing to begin with, ha! Eh? And what d'ye say to a sprang after that? And then a prick?" And with that he would spit some yellow phlegm on my belly and stretch me to breaking point.

Thus, when I came to meet Mr. Oakes again, I was not at all impressed by his superior manner. Moreover, I had remained a virgin in the technical sense, for although the leather prick had been thrust into me brutally on many occasions the shoemaker had never tried to put his own prick into me. We had agreed that my cunt was a shrine to be worshiped at but never penetrated by human member, that no semen should ever sully our shrine. For that purpose, when he saw it, he used my anus or my mouth.

One day Hazel said to me: "I want you to give this to a friend of mine, Gertie."

She handed me a letter.

"Be at the entrance to the subway at St. Enoch's Station at three this afternoon. My friend will come and ask for it."

She would say no more. I suspected at once it had something to do with Mr. Oakes. I said I would only do it if she would turn over my own bankbook to me. She finally did so after a great deal of protest.

I had been standing outside the subway for about five minutes when a shining black Rolls drew up in front of me.

Mr. Oakes leaned out of the window at the rear. He raised a finger.

"Gertrude!"

I walked slowly over to the car.

"Come for a drive," he said. "I have something to say to you."

"Is this for you?" I said, holding up the letter.

He frowned with annoyance.

"What is it?"

"A letter from Hazel. For a friend. At least that's what Hazel said."

"Of course, of course. You were sent to meet me. Now will you step in please?"

"What do you want to talk to me about?"

"We can talk about that in the car, my dear. Will you please step in?"

I did so with an air of independence which infuriated Mr. Oakes. He tapped the glass in front and gave the chauffeur his instructions.

It was some minutes before he spoke again.

"I want you to understand, Gertrude, that if you are to be of any use to me I must have absolute obedience. I thought we had made that quite clear a year ago."

Without a word I handed him the bankbook.

"What's that?" he said, the frown passing over his brow again.

"It's the money you gave me a year ago," I said evenly. "I am returning it to you. I am not a prostitute like Hazel."

Mr. Oakes misunderstood me as I had expected him to. He raised an eyebrow derisively. "I see," he said. "So you have found a boyfriend and you're in love!"

I looked out of the car window as I spoke, as though he himself were not interesting enough for my gaze. As indeed, *I was beginning to realize,* he wasn't.

"No, Mr. Oakes, I have not found a boyfriend and I am not in love, as you call it. I will never love a man. I love only one thing: *pain!* Pain is my religion and in pain I shall find my destiny, Mr. Oakes!"

I turned to look at him.

He looked startled.

This time, looking at him, I continued: "Do you not sense a change in me? Or are you insensitive? And you pretend to know what pain is! Pain purifies."

"You're too bold, Gertrude," he said at last. But I could see he was impressed. He was looking at me with new eyes. And new eyes were necessary, for in my year of pain and pitiless humiliation I had become a beauty. The curves of my body were superb. At sixteen I had the body of a young Diana of twenty.

"Too bold, Mr. Oakes?" I said with a soft smile, and, raising my skirt up over my right thigh, I said: "Look here!"

He bent over my thigh.

A permanent dark red groove encircled it completely. My shoemaker had made it for me over a period of time by twisting a thin leather thong with a piece of wood as a lever.

Mr. Oakes touched it hesitantly with his fingertips. When he looked up at me I saw fear play with lust in his eyes.

At that moment the car turned into the entrance of the big house.

"We'll see," he said shortly, and got out of the car.

I stepped out after him and followed him into the house. He led the way straight to the basement. He locked the double doors behind us.

"Your clothes," he said.

"And yours."

He nodded. We both stripped naked. He was already rampant. He moved over to me and took me in his arms. I didn't resist. He kissed me on the lips. And then, slowly, he tried to ease his cock between my thighs. I pushed him away.

"Not that," I said quietly.

He laughed. "What is to prevent my taking you?"

"Try, and see!" I said ominously.

"Gertrude," he said, changing his tone, "believe me, my dear, you are an amateur in the discipline of pain. I have had twenty years' experience. That is why I am the holder of the Holy Seal in these parts."

"The Holy Seal?"

"A small mark of distinction in our Order. It carries with it the office of Painmaster in this Lodge."

"Tell me all about the Order, Mr. Oakes!"

"I am not permitted to do that, Gertrude. What I know I cannot communicate to inferiors in the Order, and you are not even a Novice yet. You are simply what we call a Woman-Elect, a possible participant in our disciplines."

"And what's Hazel?"

"Hazel is simply a paid Whipmistress. She is not a member of the Order. She is a paid retainer."

"Is Painmaster a high office?"

"It is the highest in this part of the country. But you ask too many questions, Gertrude. And even if I wanted to answer most of them I couldn't. Even a Painmaster has no direct knowledge of the upper echelons of our Order. But perhaps you have heard enough to realize that you are a mere child, an amateur, and that you must subject yourself to my will if you are ever to be accepted as a Novice. I received instructions a few days ago that you were to be initiated if you were still found worthy."

"You mean others know of me?"

"Of course. Your name was submitted a year ago to the Holy Seat. It takes some time for the Holy Seal to be placed on the application of a Woman-Elect."

"And that's why you kept me waiting a year?"

"It was inevitable. You did right, by the way, to give me back the money. That was a prescribed test. If you had kept the money you would only have been admissible in the capacity of a retainer, a paid Whipping-girl in your case."

"Why did you try to fuck me just now, Mr. Oakes?"

He smiled.

"That, too, was a test. And I shall fuck you if you prove unworthy."

"If I prove unworthy you can fuck me any time you like."

"Good girl! I am beginning to like you, Gertrude!"

"What do we do now?"

"First, my dear Gertrude, you will flog me. You have five minutes during which time you will do your utmost to make me break down and cry for mercy. Then I shall flog you. I expect for the first time I shall have to cut you down after two minutes."

I smiled inwardly. I would show this Painmaster who I was!

"Tighten the thongs at my hands and feet," Mr. Oakes said. "There is a clock on the wall over there. When the minute hand reaches five to four start flogging with any implement you care to choose. You see them all around the walls. Stop on the dot of four."

I nodded and obeyed. I looked the implements over with a critical eye. There was nothing like my own terrible "Five-Fingered Spranger" but there was something quite like "The Prick," only it was made of thick rubber. I decided to concentrate for the whole period on his thighs and buttocks with that implement. He would not be likely to forget it!

I measured my distance and watched the clock.

Thwack! A shudder passed through his body with the first blow. It left a wide red weal on his buttocks. Thwack! Again. Again. I took my time. There was no need to tire myself. Five minutes was plenty of time. With each stroke now a little groan escaped him, but after three minutes he still hadn't screamed for mercy. He could certainly take punishment. At the end of the fourth minute he was whimpering like a little child. I put my whole weight into the last strokes, slashing the most tender part of the buttocks. With thirty seconds to go he screamed and he didn't leave off screaming until the clock struck four and I tossed the rubber prick away from me.

I helped him down gently.

He collapsed in my arms. "Brandy!" he said hoarsely, pointing to his coat. I found a flask in one of the pockets and returned with it and held it to his lips. Ten minutes passed during which I sucked his penis gently and only then was he able to stand on his feet.

"You struck hard, Gertrude," he said when he had sufficiently recovered himself.

"It would hardly have been worthwhile if I hadn't, Painmaster," I said, with a tone of mockery in my voice.

This angered him slightly. He led me by the arm over to the whipping board.

"And now we shall see if you will make a Novice!" he said.

A moment later my wrists and ankles were secured.

It was the cat-o'-nine-tails which he took up.

"Are you ready, Gertrude?"

"Yes."

I didn't flex myself. I wished to take the first stroke after the manner of virgins.

He struck and I shuddered with pleasure. He, too, took his time. After the twenty-fourth stroke a slight spittle gathered on my lips and I ceased counting. I was breathing heavily, sweating, and bleeding, but for five minutes I didn't utter a sound. He cut me down and collected me in his arms. I smiled at him and he stared back fearfully into my eyes. I could tell from his exhaustion that he had put his whole strength into the whipping. I slipped from his arms and stood naked before him. He hesitated, and then, falling to his knees, he thrust his head and mouth upwards between my thighs. I allowed him to suck away the slime and sweat and then, grasping him by the hairs of his head, I thrust him away from me.

"No, Painmaster," I said gently. "I didn't scream. I felt no agony of dying. You are not worthy to lick my cunt!" I stood back and kicked him in the face with my bare foot. He fell on the straw. "Tell your betters I have come," I said.

I put my clothes on, unlocked the double doors and left the big house.

Two nights later, when I was alone in the flat, someone knocked at the door. I opened it. A man who looked like a tramp stood on the threshold.

"I am looking for Gertrude Gault," he said.

"I am Gertrude Gault," I replied.

"I was to recognize her by a mark on her thigh."

I pulled up my skirt and showed the mark.

"Are you alone?"

I nodded.

"Can I come in?"

I allowed him to enter. He looked around the room in disgust.

"You will not be allowed to live here much longer," he said.

"Who are you?"

"That's not important," he said. "I come on high authority. I have been instructed to mark you with the Holy Seal."

"What does that mean?"

"It means that you have been appointed Painmistress for this part of the country."

I gasped. "What about Oakes?"

"The Painmaster is dead," the stranger said. "He committed suicide two nights ago. He nominated you as his successor. The Holy Seat cabled its confirmation today. It is my duty to put the seal on you." He became business-like. "Are we likely to be disturbed?"

"How long will it take?"

"Fifteen minutes at the most."

I walked over and locked the door.

"Your skirt," he said, "and whatever you wear under it. Then sit on the table."

I exposed myself for him.

He worked quickly.

First a needle with which he pierced the right lip of my sex. It was not at all painful. He had great dexterity, and with his little bottle of alcohol and cotton wool he was scrupulously clean. Next he passed a gold ring, about the thickness of a wedding ring, through it. This was more painful. I shut my eyes and absorbed the sensation, coveting it. The cross of polished black stone which he now hung from the ring was not heavy. It weighed perhaps an ounce or two. Then he sealed the two rings, the one which passed through the right lip and the one which passed through the top of the cross with a kind of gold metal compound which he sealed with a tiny stamp. I couldn't make out the figuration at that distance. And then it was over. He stood back and replaced his instruments in his raincoat pocket.

"Your official inauguration will take place in two weeks' time," he said. "But Mr. Prentice, whom you have already met, will get in touch with you before that. He will explain to you exactly all the duties and privileges of your office. And now, I had better go."

As he spoke the last words there suddenly came a rattling at the door.

"Who locked this bliddy door! Open up this bliddy door!"

"Who's that?" the stranger whispered.

I was transfixed with fear.

"It's my father, Razor King!"

"Your skirt, quick!" the stranger hissed.

I stepped into it quickly. But what did that matter? With the locked door my father would think the worst anyway. He might even use his razors!

"Open up this bliddy door before ah break it down!"

I flashed a glance at the stranger. He nodded towards the door. I slipped across the room and opened it.

My father burst in like a gorilla. He reeked of drink and he had a plump black-haired tart with him.

He stared first at me and then at the stranger.

The woman with him had stopped giggling. She guessed that there was going to be violence.

"Who the bliddy hell are you!"

"I came to see you, Razor King," the stranger said.

"Aye! A likely story! And that's why ye locked the bliddy door on me!"

"I asked your daughter to lock the door because I didn't want to be seen by anybody but you. It would be dangerous if too many people saw us together."

"What the bliddy hell are you talkin about? Dangerous!"

The stranger took two five-pound notes from his pocket and laid them on the table which stood between himself and my father.

"Do you want to talk business or don't you!" he snapped.

My father stared at the money, then at me, and then back at the stranger.

"We need a man to do a job," the stranger said. "A man who's not afraid of a fight."

"Who's we?"

"You'll meet the boss next week," the stranger said. "If you'll come to the corner of Jamaica Street and Clyde Street next Friday evening about seven we'll tell you exactly what it's all about." He pushed the two notes towards my father. "Meanwhile you can take that on account."

My father hesitated only momentarily. Then he took the notes and stuffed them into his trouser pocket.

Suddenly he looked sly.

"An whit if ah say ah don't believe ye? Whit if ah wis tae say ah know whit ye were doin here with ma daughter? Whit if ah wis tae bash yer heed in fer ye!"

"You'd be a fool," the stranger replied, calmly. "People who can pay our kind of money are dangerous. You'd lose money and you'd end up stiff in the river."

It was the wrong thing to say to Razor King when he was drunk.

"We'll see who's dangerous!" Razor King snarled, and whipped one of his big razors out of his pocket.

Simultaneously the stranger produced an ugly black automatic.

"One wrong move from you, Gault, and I'll shoot you in the belly."

Razor King, the open razor in his hand, stared at the gun. A look of dawning comprehension passed over his heavy features. In that confined space he wouldn't stand a dog's chance. The man would shoot him dead before he had moved a foot. He closed the razor and said in a wheedling tone: "This job you were talkin aboot? How much would there be in it fer me?"

"Twenty more next Friday, and forty when you've done the job."

"Ah'll be there," Razor King said. "Now get oot before ah change ma mind and mark ye!"

The stranger did so, quietly and efficiently, covering Razor King with the gun until he was right outside the door. Razor King kicked the door shut with his foot. He stared at me for a moment, and then, remembering the money in his pocket, his ill-humor left him. He winked at the woman.

"Let's go on oot an get a wee drink first!" he said.

They left a minute after the stranger.

With a sigh of relief I sat down on the cot.

☙

With Johnnie it had to happen.

I never knew whether Hazel had received instructions. But that doesn't matter.

During Razor King's periodic drunken bouts Hazel was alone with Johnnie. He still sat watching her. She would be washing at the sink, or putting on her silk stockings, or brushing her hair. We all—Hazel, Johnnie and myself—saw it coming. Johnnie was waiting. But for some time now he had bothered less to conceal his desire.

But still he waited.

And then, a few days after the visit of the stranger, he made his first overt move. Did Hazel force it?

Johnnie reached out with his hand and caught Hazel by the wrist. The choice was still Hazel's. If she had freed herself Johnnie would probably have been content to wait. As she stared into his eyes the knowledge came to her that he would do as she wished him to do. His eyes appraised her, posed a question. And Hazel smiled.

"You'll be awa' oot, Gertie."

I realized at once what it meant.

That night Hazel became Johnnie's mistress.

From then on it was a question of days.

Razor King, habitually drunk now, took Hazel as a bull takes a cow. And sometimes Ella was there, too. That was the dark woman. The one who had giggled. The King took them both to bed, the one giggling, the other cool.

Johnnie watched.

And then, towards the end of the week, on the Saturday night before the fatal Sunday, he told Hazel that she would not sleep with his father again. Hazel, responding passionately, held him tightly in her arms, and I wondered as she did so what she was doing and why she did it, for I knew she loved neither man. I knew it was not her intention to remain for long in the squalor of the Gorbals, even as its queen. It occurred to me then, and it must have occurred to Hazel a long time before, that as strong as these men were, my father, the wolf of the slums, and men like him, there were others in the city who could crush them by lifting a telephone. Neither Johnnie nor my father would ever have admitted that, and as long as they inhabited the narrow world of violence in the Gorbals, as long as they did not approach on the wider, more profitable territory of the city at large, the truth would never be forced upon them. The situation in the Gorbals was tolerated because it did not threaten city interests. Thus, Hazel's reality was the reality of neither man. She had grown up amongst them, despising them, accepting for the present the love of the strongest, making plans for an entirely different future to begin at the moment she was free to choose. Perhaps it was because she knew that that moment was about to arrive that she accepted Johnnie as a lover. And the idea of certain conflict fascinated her.

"Keep yer bliddy hauns aff her!"

To see Razor King sway in the doorway, his face a mask of anger and incomprehension, his huge hands tense as a strangler's, caused an electric sensation that was almost lust to move in me. I backed away, near Hazel, leaving the center of the floor vacant for the two men.

"Jist keep yer big bliddy hauns aff Hazel!" Johnnie repeated.

Razor King lurched towards him with an oath.

Johnnie was quick but he had underestimated my father's strength and it was brute force that counted in that confined space. Johnnie tried hard to hold Razor King in the full-nelson, but the older man stiffened, ducked with a grunt, making a butt of his bottom, and hurled himself backwards with his full power. They crashed together on the floor, Gault's body like a sack of sand knocking all the breath out of his son. And then Razor King was up and as Johnnie struggled to his feet my father's boot took him heavily on the mouth so that Johnnie's head struck backwards with a sickening thud on the floor. He didn't move after that.

Hazel slipped quickly into bed, accepting Johnnie's defeat with equanimity.

Johnnie crawled out some time during the night, leaving Hazel in his father's arms.

But in the morning I knew even before Allison came. I had been out as usual for milk and the Sunday papers. I saw the crowd collect. I even saw the razor thrown from the third story window. I knew that it would take place that morning in the open street.

Less than two hours later my father was dead.

The Painmistress

"Take me to the big house, Hazel."

It was two hours since the police and the ambulances had left. Hazel was sitting staring out of the dirty window at the street. The Gorbals would be quiet for the rest of the day.

"What?"

"I want you to take me to the big house. There's no point in staying on here now."

"Don't be silly, Gertie, I can't just take you there. I have to wait for orders."

"You'll be taking orders from me in the future," I said. "Didn't they tell you?"

"Tell me what?"

"Oakes is dead. Didn't you know that?"

"Yes, I heard," she said quietly. "And I know more than that. Imagine, some woman is to be Painmistress!"

"What's wrong with that?"

"What's right with it!" Hazel said. "Oh, I could handle Oakes! He liked a bit on the side now and again. I got on well with him, specially once he knew I was with

Razor King. He liked the idea of that, having the King's woman, I mean."

She got up.

"Is there a cup of tea, Gertie?"

"I'm the woman, Hazel."

It still didn't seem to register.

"But a woman, imagine that! Probably some old bitch that wants her tits bitten off!"

She had gone over to the fire. She shook the kettle to see if there was water in it.

I took off my skirt.

"Look, Hazel!"

She turned. "What the . . ." And then she stopped. She was staring at the black cross. "Where did you get that?" she whispered.

"You know what it is?"

"It's the Holy Seal!"

"Yes," I said. "And I am the new Painmistress. Now, will you take me to the big house?"

ह§

"Gertrude!"

Harry Prentice hurried across the room and kissed my hand. He nodded to Hazel.

"You'd better wait here," he said to her. We were in the big reception room. "And if you don't mind, Gertrude, I'd like you to come with me."

I followed him into a large comfortably furnished library where a fire blazed in the open hearth. He sat down opposite me.

"I was going to get in touch with you in the middle of the week," he said, "but now you're here it's just as well. What brings you?"

I told him of the fatal battle.

"I see," he said. "So really, you don't need to go back now. That's just as well too. Since I spoke to the special Nuncio I've been worried about you. Your father was a dangerous man."

"Nuncio?"

"Yes. The man who put the Holy Seal on you, a kind of traveling ambassador from the Holy Seat itself. He has returned to Madrid."

"Madrid!"

"Yes. The Holy Seat is in Madrid, Gertrude, but I have a great deal to explain to you, so it would be better if you listened for a while."

I nodded.

"First, about myself," Harry said. "As you know, I was Mr. Oakes's secretary. But it wasn't in a private capacity. I am a Permanent Secretary to the Holy Seal. Thus, I am automatically your secretary, for it is you who now bears the Holy Seal. I am now entirely at your disposal as a counselor and servant. It is my job to make you entirely conversant with the duties and privileges of your office and to be always at your side to advise and help you.

"Now, I must tell you something of the organization of the Order. At the head of the Order, in the Holy Seat at Madrid, is the Holy Pain Father. His identity, like the identities of most of the members of the upper echelon, is not known to me. Under him, forming the Central Executive

93

Committee, are the twelve Pain Cardinals. They have a position roughly equivalent to that of the Cardinals in the Roman Church. They meet in conclave to elect the Holy Pain Father, who is most often referred to simply as Pain. Each Pain Cardinal has six Grand Painmasters under him, and they in turn have each twelve Painmasters or Pain-mistresses under them. Thus, you see that you are one of eight hundred and sixty-four Painmasters or Pain-mistresses. In your present capacity the nearest you will come to the Holy Seat is to have direct contact with your own Grand Painmaster, Sir William L. . ., who will be present at your official inauguration. Then there is the Permanent Secretariat, of which I am a member. We have only that authority delegated to us by you, the true mem-

bers of the Hierarchy. If you were chosen as a Grand Painmistress while I was still in your service, you would have the choice of taking me with you as your secretary or of accepting the secretary of the ex-Grand Painmaster. In one sense his services would be an advantage since he would be already acquainted with all the customary forms pertaining to his master's office, but that can be learned and I don't suppose it's necessary to point out to you that a man who has risen with you is likely to prove more loyal.

"Then, there are various Nuncios, one of whom you met the other night. They are the private Messengers of Pain and hold a kind of honorary position within the Hierarchy.

"After that, there are any number of paid retainers. Hazel is one of them. She is a Whipmistress. Theoretically, her services can be dispensed with at any time, but if that decision were taken it would be necessary to do away with her because she knows too much. Once she had the honor of whipping Sir William L . . . himself, for example.

"Finally, there is the main body of ordinary members, the Members of Pain. The gentlemen you met here on your first visit were in that category. There are the Novices, and from time to time Men or Women-Elect, as they are called. You became automatically a Woman-Elect after your first visit here. Under normal circumstances you would have become a Novice at the next General Meeting. But before his death, Mr. Oakes set out his reasons carefully and persuasively for recommending you to the Office of Painmistress. Sir William was evidently convinced and got in touch at once with his Pain Cardinal. That's all I know."

He got up and poured himself a drink.

"Would you like one, Gertrude?"

I nodded.

When he handed it to me, he said: "I agreed with Mr. Oakes. I think you are just what is needed to bring discipline back to the Order in this area."

I smiled and thanked him.

"If you have any questions?" he said.

"I have," I said. "Does this house belong to me?"

"As long as you are Painmistress."

"What about money?"

"You needn't worry about expense," he said with a smile. "You have a rich Congregation."

"Will they like me?"

"They will obey you."

"Can I choose new retainers if I wish to?"

"Of course."

"I know a man."

"Ah, you have one in mind?"

"My personal Whipmaster," I said. "A Glasgow cobbler. It was he who groomed me to be what I am."

"Excellent! We should employ him at once!"

"Tomorrow I shall fetch him. I'll want you to come with me."

"Gladly, my Lady!"

"I like you, Harry."

"I like you, Gertrude!"

I smiled at him. "Why did you call me 'my Lady'?"

"In public, Gertrude, I shall always call you that in the future. We must preserve the dignities of the Order. Mr. Oakes had become too lax. Many suspected it. You, Gertrude, must be a disciplinarian from the beginning."

ॐ

I watched the cars arrive from my private apartment on the top floor of the big house, Rolls-Royces, Daimlers, Talbots, and many others. Two uniformed attendants were directing the parking. Harry had already gone downstairs and I assumed he was occupying himself with the more important guests among the Members, for, of course, I found out at once that our Order, like all earthly orders, admitted of privileges for the rich and powerful. Harry had explained a great deal of this to me. Mr. Oakes had been a millionaire. Sir William L. . . . was a great landowner. How then had I been chosen? In what way could I enrich or bring power to the Order? All

Harry could say was that Oakes himself had on more than one occasion referred to this kind of corruption within the Order, to its being spoilt by wealth and privilege, to the possibility of its degenerating into a private club in which the wealthy could indulge in petty obscenities, and it was Harry's opinion that a stricture must have come from the Holy Seat itself, both to Sir William L. . . and, perhaps through him, to Oakes, for at no time, Harry said, had either man impressed him as possessing a holy zeal for the commission of their trust. There was too much amusement, too many gatherings which were merely lascivious, too much hiring of professional exhibitionists from without the Order, couples who would dance in the nude and copulate at the same time, sleek-bodied women of various races and preferably of Lesbian tendencies who would rub and lick each other's sex for the delight of Members; in fact, in Harry's opinion, and that seemed to be borne out by the fact that those Members who actively participated in flagellation were becoming fewer and fewer in number, the big house was in danger of degenerating into a profitable brothel. There, he suspected, was the reason for my election. Indeed, Oakes's last letter to his Grand Painmaster, Sir William L. . ., had hinted at this. New blood was needed in a decadent sect. "More blood," Harry said with a smile, "more blood and less titivation." It seemed that our Congregation had swollen to two hundred members and that not five percent of those members had appeared more than once for flagellation.

All this worried me as I watched the Members arrive in their fine cars. How on earth would I be able to control two hundred idle and lascivious men and women, some of whom, according to Harry, were very prominent in public affairs in this part of the country! What if they refused to obey me? How could I hope, in one night, to clear away all the corruption which my predecessor had allowed to come to exist during the ten years of his office? What if I was faced with mutiny? Harry had done his best to console me. He would be there at my right hand. Every one of the two hundred had sworn to obey under the penalty of Excommunication, and that, in the Order of Pain, meant death. Again, some Members would be firmly on my side. Mr. Bing for example, and Mr. Duval, and the redoubtable Mr. Coldstream. And, I was not to forget that Sir William L. . . would be present, incognito of course, for none of the Members knew him except as an ordinary Member. No, in Harry's opinion, my Congregation would obey.

But would it ?

I had no means of knowing in advance.

"Is everything ready, Willie?" I said.

Willie, who had been reading the evening paper, looked up. "Aye," he said.

The flogging room in the basement had been altered. Willie himself had attended to the installation of the new fixtures. The whipping board had been removed. Metal rings had been sunk into the floor and ceiling. Victims would now be stretched as I had been when I delivered myself over to Willie's doting punishment in the back shop of the bootmaker's in Cumberland Street.

New instruments had been provided. No expense had been spared. Somehow Willie's company was a great comfort to me. Here was a Whippingmaster of imagination. He was to have his own will with any female member of our organization; to whip, to suck, to dote, to bring religion where religion had not been before. But his loyalty touched me. It was my body which interested him. And it was his. Before all the world, it was his.

For some time now no more cars had arrived. If that meant that everyone had already come then Harry would soon be sending for me. I pulled up my skirt and lay over a soft leather stool in front of Willie.

"Whip me a little, Willie!" I breathed.

He took a three-pronged leather strap from his pocket and with his full force gave me six cruel blows across the soft, sweat-smeared surface of my buttocks. And then his nose and tongue were there, nudging, exploring. I raised my palpitating rump so that my slimy cunt came in contact with his darting wet tongue, and to feel it there, at my body's center, strong, hard, and masterful, just that, gave me back the knowledge of my own power, the religious certainty of my commitment.

Someone knocked at the door.

Willie got up and I slipped off the stool.

"Come in!"

It was Harry.

"They've come, Gertrude!"

"All?"

He nodded. "It's time you put in an appearance. They're all anxious to see you."

"Where have you put them?"

"In the Temple."

I nodded.

The Temple was a large, sparsely furnished hall at the back of the house, its ceiling domed like that of a mosque. There was a pulpit, and beside it a large whipping block. Chairs were arranged as in a church, in three segments with two aisles running between. Behind the pulpit and dominating the whole auditorium was a sculpted version of the picture I had first seen in the reception room, the *Virgin Death*.

"I shall come now. Go and prepare them."

He bowed and went out.

Willie helped me to dress in the plain toga of black cloth. Underneath, apart from a chain of iron drawn tightly about my waist and the black cross which fell from my cunt against the soft white surface of my right thigh, I was stark naked. My nipples and my navel had been treated with mascara. I stepped into my leather thong sandals and wound my soft black hair out of sight under a tall black turban.

"Be near, Willie," I said just before I went out.

There was a trapdoor in the pulpit so that the bearer of the Holy Seal could appear suddenly and impressively among the Congregation.

A moment later I was standing high in the pulpit, a green arc light directed skillfully at me, and below me in the auditorium a complete silence reigned.

I could see the white faces craning up towards me, old faces, young faces, handsome faces, ugly faces, tired faces, fat faces, thin faces, gaunt faces, all alight with anticipation. Out of the corner of my eye I could see Harry, wearing a black mask across the upper part of his face, standing naked and rampant, and Willie, the Whippingmaster at his block. I raised my arms, my long fingers distended, making an impressive cross of my body.

"I am Gertrude!"

"She is Gertrude!" Harry echoed in a deeper voice.

"I am the bearer of the Holy Seal!"

"She is the bearer of the Holy Seal!"

"I am come to live amongst you as Pain!"

"She is come to live amongst us as Pain!"

Hazel, behind the wings, struck across her quivering buttocks at that moment by the five-fingered spranger, let out a bloodcurdling scream of agony.

When that died away I spoke again to the sea of white, straining faces.

"I am Gertrude!"

"She is Gertrude!"

"I am your Painmistress!"

"She is our Painmistress!"

"I am Mistress and Minister to your pain!"

"She is Mistress and Minister to our pain!"

I looked down to the front row and my eyes singled out a plump but pretty well-dressed woman who sat next to an impressive-looking man with a military moustache.

I pointed my finger at her. She cringed closer to her escort.

"Stand up, woman!" I said.

She hesitated. Her escort looked indignant. But after a few seconds she shifted nervously to her feet. She was really quite beautiful in spite of the slight plumpness. She would be about thirty-five, I guessed. I could imagine the soft white flesh, tremulous and slightly damp under her fashionable dress.

"You are a Member?"

"Yes . . . my Lady!"

I smiled and stretched out my hand towards her.

"Come," I said gently. "For my first Mass I have chosen you to perform the Rite of the Virgin Death!"

A wondering murmur ran through the auditorium. I knew why. Harry had told me that the corruption in our Congregation extended even to the holiest of rituals so that for this particular Rite, Mr. Oakes had been in the habit of employing a professional to be whipped on the block below the sculpted passion of death. Thus, my command struck deep at corrupt usage, especially as I had chosen a woman from the front row, that's to say, one who was probably a celebrity or the wife of a celebrity in the outside world.

"I . . ." Her gaze broke with mine and she glanced at her escort. He was already on his feet and he looked furious.

"Come!" I repeated, ignoring him.

She still hesitated.

The man spoke. He was furious but his voice was restrained.

"Excuse me, my Lady, but this is not the usual practice in our Congregation. My wife . . . "

"*Silence! In this Temple she is not your wife, nor are you your own master, sir! You are the creatures of Pain and by your obedience Pain will judge you! Sit down, sir, before you offend mortally!*"

I raised my right hand—a beam of white light fell on the gentleman's face.

"Lord E. . .," Harry's deep voice intoned, "you will obey the Seal!"

The woman, terrified, made as if to come forward, but her husband gripped her by the wrist. He turned to face a thin gray-haired man who sat quietly at the end of the front row.

"What have you to say to this, Sir William! It's an outrage!"

"I, Lord E. . . ?" Sir William said in a hushed tone. "What should I have to say?"

"Can you not control this upstart?" Lord E. . . demanded.

I realized at once that Lord E. . . knew Sir William's identity within the Order. Corruption, it seemed, had spread far. I glanced at Harry. He too had understood and his eyes flickered dangerously behind his mask.

"I . . ." Sir William stammered, coming to his feet.

"Silence!" I cried. I pointed an accusing finger at Sir William. "Sit down, sir, or to Pain you will answer!"

Sir William flopped back into his seat, a broken man. I clapped my hands. Two masked men appeared suddenly. They were dressed in black tights and black turtle-necked pullovers. They moved like ballet-dancers.

I pointed to Lord E. . .

"Take that blasphemous rogue to the cellars!" I commanded.

Lord E. . . gasped and was about to speak, but one of my men in black had produced a short length of lead piping. He struck Lord E. . . once, hard, across the cheek-bone, and the gentleman collapsed in their arms. Then, swiftly, they removed the unconscious body.

Harry, meanwhile, had descended from beside the block and was dragging Lady E. . . towards the dais by the wrist. The rest of the company were shocked. Half of them were standing up.

"*Members, be seated. You are in the presence of Pain!*" This was blared through the auditorium as if by megaphone. Harry and I had arranged a number of these stage effects against any eventuality. The reaction was instantaneous. The audience sat down.

"Now let us have silence!" I cried.

The hall was silent.

"Strip naked!" I said to Lady E . . .

She hastened to obey.

Her slightly fat, milkwhite breasts sprang free of her brassiere like startling rubber balls. The soft fat on her shoulders and upper arms was pink and quivering. In silence she undressed, removing her girdle so that the soft flesh of her creamy belly fell in a tremulous melon-smooth disc over her thick-chevroned cunt. She stood shyly before the multitude.

I raised my arms to form a cross of my body once more.

"Let us pray!" I said.

The Congregation went on to its knees.

"To thee, oh Pain, we consecrate the agony of this woman's flesh! Help her to suffer! To feel the quick brightness of your movement in all the muscle and fiber! Teach her to scream! Teach her to treasure every humiliation, every violence that we, thy servants, inflict upon her trembling flesh! Take unto thyself her utmost misery and turn it by the shard of thy cruel tongue into the fire of purity in her veins! Amen."

I turned to Willie.

"Let us proceed."

He bound her tightly with leather thongs to the block so that her large spreading buttocks jutted out like marble towards him. Her big creamy thighs were thonged a foot apart at the knees so that her anus showed like a small red berry peeping beneath darkling hair and the stubborn tuft of her hot cunt was visible from the rear.

I raised my right hand.

"Let the Great Lord of Pain visit the willing flesh of this trembling woman with his dark power, and let all Communicants who visit this, the symbol and flesh of our Virgin of Death, with the seal of their doting lips be themselves visited with an eternal lust for his quick and striking fire!"

I turned to the Members.

"Let the Communicants come forward!"

The Members rose as one body. They formed silent queues in the aisles.

"Let the first Member bring his lips to the altar!"

And then they were moving, each member kneeling in front of the soft mellow buttocks, crossing himself, and sinking his tongue to the hilt in the hair-sharded little red anus of the lovely Lady E. . . .

This part of the ceremony took about half an hour because of the large number of Communicants. At the end of it Lady E. . . was shuddering with lust. She had no doubt come two or three times during the sacrament. The Communicants had returned in silence to their seats.

"Daughter! Are you ready to receive the visitation of Pain himself?"

"Yes, oh yes! Please!" Lady E. . . gasped.

I nodded to Willie.

He stepped back into position and struck her forcibly on the buttocks with the brand new five-fingered spranger. I noticed that the wood of the block was wet with Lady E. . .'s sweat. After the third stroke it seemed as though her quivering flesh was trying to melt into the wood.

At the sixth stroke she screamed and the terrible scream ran like nightmare amongst the members. Their faces were tense and receptive.

I directed Willie to go on. His big member flapped rampant on his gleaming white belly as he struck.

The scream came again.

He struck again.

At the tenth stroke I recognized the familiar scream out of control. The sacrament was accomplished. The lady was "beside herself": only then did she enter pure into religion. I threw off my black vestments and stepped naked down from the pulpit, the black cross swinging between my legs.

I motioned Willie aside and fell on my knees before the bleeding buttocks. Skillfully I ran my tongue in the sweating furrow of her cunt until I felt the shudder of response from her whole torso. Then, kneeling straight up, I crossed myself and turned again to face the members. The green arc light had followed me and gave a ghostly radiance to the full curves of my flesh. I raised my naked arms so that my breasts were lifted high, my black nipples poised delicately like the eyes of an insect.

"Holy Father of Pain, we thank thee!" I screamed. "May the Virgin Death be appeased by this, her sacrament!"

In unison the Members said, *Amen.*

Willie cut the woman from the block and she was carried out by the two men in black.

I returned to the pulpit.

The most difficult part of the ceremony was over. One of the most influential women had accepted public flagellation. True, I still had to deal with her husband, who was locked in the cellars, but for them, the Members, he had already been dealt with. My authority was established. Harry, his arms crossed on his broad chest, and his own member still rampant, stood below the pulpit to the right, facing them. I looked over the sea of faces and spoke calmly.

"Members of Pain! I speak to you now to recall you to your true discipline! Over the years you have become fat and idle and prurient. Instead of lacerating your own flesh you have preferred to lacerate the flesh of hired minions, instead of knowing the joy of Pain you have inflicted an unholy pain on prostitutes, instead of drinking at the well of suffering you have come drunk, fat, and replete with earthly joys to make a brothel of your Holy Temple. You have made an idol of ordinary lust and come amused to exercise it in the Holy Temple of Pain! With your money and your earthly power you have bribed and corrupted Pain's holy servants and caused the sense of Order and Hierarchy in this Congregation to resemble an auction in a whorehouse! The repercussions of your blasphemous behavior are not yet at an end. But the Order of Pain will weed all corruption out. Men may die, but the Order is everlasting!

"Did you think that Pain was so weak that He would continue to overlook this outrage?

"Did you think you had bought Him too?

"Let me warn you of your error here and now! Rather would Pain thrust redhot steel through each and every cowardly heart in this Congregation than suffer your blasphemies any longer! It is for you, the Members, to choose: *Death or Purification!* I warn you to beware! *I*, bearing the Holy Seal, am the Judgment!"

I changed my tone of voice: "All Members in the first two rows will now leave the Temple. They will follow the Whippingmaster to the Room of Flagellation. They will taste great Pain tonight!"

I fell silent until these chosen twenty had been ushered out of the Temple.

When they had gone I addressed those who remained.

"I take it that the twenty Members who have just gone to their punishment were at the center of the corruption of which I spoke. That does not exonerate you. When you felt the wind of corruption in our Holy Order you should have taken a firm stand against it. For this reason you will each of you, during the next three months, make a weekly presentation of his flesh for flagellation. Only the dead will be excused. And now, before you go, you will each of you swear allegiance to me, your Holy Painmistress, by kissing my cunt."

I came down out of the pulpit and stood, hands on hips, my mound thrust forwards, to meet the first of a hundred and eighty doting tongues.

సౌ

In my private apartment I sat naked in front of the fire. From time to time I touched my clitoris and allowed the heat from the glowing embers to strike softly on the wet red amorphousness which lined the interior of my cunt.

To have a cunt!

How wonderful it was to be possessed of this sensitive passage! And yet, as I sat there fingering it, I knew that it would never know the presence of a male member. The office of Painmistress did not require me to be a virgin, nor any other position in the Holy Hierarchy. I knew that now. But I remembered poor Oakes saying that he hoped I would turn out to be "our Virgin." The thought rankled. What had he meant? Was it not enough to be Painmistress? Could I not hope soon to be a Grand Painmistress, even a Pain Cardinal? Why then should I not give myself to Harry when he came up, Harry whose big cock I had sucked innumerable times since I had arrived definitively in the big house. Harry, whose balls I had caressed, bringing them gently against my wet, lustful lips? Of all the men I had known, Harry was the most worthy. Why not, then? He could sleep with me. I would be his woman. And as a Whippingmaster he was excellent. Why not? Why?

I had not bothered to join Harry and Willie in the basement. Lord E. . . was securely locked in the cellar humorously referred to as the "death-cell." His wife was recovering in one of the many antechambers. The twenty proud Members were at present being reduced in the flagellation room to so much whining flesh. I had already sent instructions that they were to be detained for a week's continual treatment. By the time they went back to their ordinary lives they would have signed and re-signed allegiance with their blood.

What was it then that haunted me? Why was I not satisfied with the success of my official inauguration?

Was it that I was not born to be a member of the Hierarchy? What strange lust made me cling to my virginity?

Above the fire was the usual picture representing the Virgin Death.

The Virgin Death?

Had I to die a virgin?

How?

Like her?

Nailed to a cross of wood?

A sweat of lust had gathered about my thighs.

To be crucified?

Was that the ambition that lurked in my heart?

The last dedication?

Life itself?

For the Order?

Why, then, had they elected me? No, not death, not that ultimate leap into nothingness. Pain, yes. Pain and more pain. But where did that lead if not to death? Death, the final pain. And if death, why not the Virgin Death?

Had she ever existed?

Our Virgin, Oakes had said. What did he mean? I lifted the black cross between my fingers. What did it mean? Why had they attached it to me like a price-ticket to a sold object? To whom could I go for advice? To Sir William? The Grand Painmaster! But he was part of the corruption! He was what I had been brought in to destroy. To whom then? Harry? But Harry for all his intelligence and bodily beauty was only a functionary. What could he tell me? He was absolutely cut off from the higher echelons of the Order, like Oakes. Like Sir William? Perhaps he, already corrupt, could be persuaded to give me information.

I smiled at the thought.

My own Grandmaster was at present in the cellars undergoing the same punishment as the mutinous Members! And he had not raised his voice in protest. Neither had Bing, who was also amongst the twenty, nor Duval, nor Coldstream, but those three were evidently to be trusted. That's to say, in so far as anyone in our Congregation could be trusted.

Try as I would, I could not kill the little worm of discontent that wriggled deep within me. Before my election I had, as it were, been innocent, involved entirely in my personal pain and the ecstasy of my flesh. I had had no contact with intrigue, with politics; my religion was pure. I could remember loving St. Francis as a small child, but the worldly machinations of the Popes and Cardinals had held no interest for me. And here now, in another Order, an Order similar in structure to that of the Roman one, I was already established within the Hierarchy. Was this, then, to be my life? Perhaps in the distant future to be elected Pain Cardinal and to have a voice in the election of Pain?

I rolled over on my soft belly on the rug and closed my eyes. There was a delicious tiredness at my limbs. It had been a strenuous day. I had emerged victorious. Time enough later to think of the small needle of discontent.

There was a knock at the door.

"Come in!"

It was Harry.

"All over," he said as he walked across to the fire and sat cross-legged beside me. "Your Willie did a good job. I'm sure half the women are in love with him already."

"What about Hazel?"

"They've gone to bed together."

"Who?"

"Willie and Hazel. They make a good pair!"

I felt a small prick of jealousy, but it soon faded. What did it matter? Those innocent days could never be recaptured.

"Something worrying you?"

Harry had laid his hand on my buttocks and was caressing them gently. I turned over so that my hot hairy mound came against his hand.

"Why don't I give myself to you, Harry?"

He was slightly pale.

"Why don't you?" he said. "You know I worship you, Gertrude."

His fingers played gently with my pubic hairs and touched the sensitive skin of my inner thighs. He lifted the black cross and looked at it as he might have looked at a pocket watch.

"You're not happy," he said, looking at me intensely.

"No."

My eyes were closed. I felt his warm palm on my belly.

"You want to get away from all this?"

I laughed sadly, opening my eyes to look at him. His face was set. He was not wearing his spectacles.

"Get away?" I said softly. "What does that mean? You know there is no way out of the Order, Harry."

He did not answer.

"You think there is?"

"We could disappear," he said in a dull voice. "We could, Gertrude. We could go somewhere where they would never find us . . ."

I laid my hand on his, causing his hand to lie heavily on my belly.

"Do you really think so, Harry? Do people like us not need the Order? Is that not why we belong to it?"

"I don't," he said obstinately. "Of course, I'm not a member of the Hierarchy. I'm simply a permanent civil servant!"

"Would you make me happy, Harry?"

"Yes, Gertrude. I think I would!"

"And if I wanted one day to be flogged to death?"

He was deadly pale.

"Could you not learn ordinary love, Gertrude? I mean not ordinary! But a man and woman love."

"You mean ordinary love, Harry," I said gently.

He smiled hopelessly.

"Yes. That's what I mean."

"No, Harry. I'm afraid. Don't think I don't want you just now. But afterwards. What then?"

"But the Order is not against our making love, Gertrude! And afterwards—so what? Afterwards, when we feel like it, we make love again. What else?"

"It sounds monotonous, Harry. I couldn't bear for it to become monotonous."

"But life's like that, Gertrude! What do you want? You can't burn with passion all the time. You would soon burn yourself out. Like phosphorous."

"Perhaps that's the answer," I said quietly.

"What do you mean?"

"To raise passion to such a level that life becomes extinct within it."

"But that's suicide, Gertrude!"

"I've been thinking, Harry."

"What about?"

"About the Virgin Death. Do you know anything about that?"

"Of course. She symbolizes the infinite lust for Pain, to the point of death."

"Did she exist?"

"Oh, lots of people have died under flagellation," he said evasively. "We had a stockbroker ourselves who went out with a heart attack during a flogging."

"Yes, but it's not the same, Harry. This woman mounted the cross to die. She knew she was going to die. She demanded it. Did she exist?"

"I suppose from the official standpoint she did. But we're living in the twentieth century, Gertrude. It's a relative age. People don't have the same lust for the infinite, or if they do they're mad. What's the point? Men like to be flogged or to flog. But to the point of death, that's another thing."

"But that's just the point, Harry. You know the point at which one screams out of control, the point at which one is simply a will-less victim of the thongs? That is dying, Harry, when one no longer has the power of will. You are suspended in Pain; you no longer wish for it to go on or stop. You become Pain. If someone were to drive a knife into your heart at that moment, you wouldn't feel it;

it would be like turning off the light, that's all. Normally, when you don't die, you come back through Pain to yourself, and it is you who is painful, your own aching flesh. And there's nothing in that; it's simply painful. The triumph is in the rising beyond the painful into Pain. Once that leap out of the self has been made, it is an anticlimax to go back. That's like ordinary lust which goes on and on. You come to the climax and then everything is shattered. You are yourself again, alone, just as you were before. And it goes on, and on, and on. Until we feel like it again, you said a moment ago. But that's monotonous, Harry. And it's the same with flagellation. Only with flagellation there's no excuse. It's sheer cowardice to come back. Only that person is admirable, only that person is truly religious who has the courage not to come back. What for, after all? To do it all over again?"

"All right," Harry said in a tired voice, "so you choose to die because you find life monotonous, because it goes on and on with the same rising and falling, the same thrills which are provoked and which come to an end. But that is what living is, Gertrude, and I don't see why one should expect it to be anything else. For me the courageous thing to do is to come to terms with what you call monotony, that's to say with reality, to accept it, and intelligently alter it to one's best advantage. Your way out is sheer Nihilism, and there's a strong core of Nihilism in all the religions. You call life meaningless, and you think you assert your freedom in rejecting it. But your act of suicide is just as meaningless as any other. And the application of the word *meaningful,* or *purposive,* to life in the abstract is itself meaningless. All meanings and purposes are men's meanings and purposes; men choose them; often courageously, and then living is easier, but it is the living that counts; death is nothing; it is simply the point at which there is no more possibility. It may or may not be courageous to court death, but for me it's insane."

"Oh Harry!" I said, turning once again onto my belly, "if only I could accept the tepid thing you call living! I want to give myself to you. Believe me! I do!"

"Do so, then! Why this eternal search for a meaning! Take life as it comes! Accept the thrills. Don't question their meaning. They have no more meaning than a rose's redness. In terms of what, for God's sake, do you want to justify a fuck!"

I laughed, sat up, and kissed him gently on the lips. His arms encircled my naked body at once and pulled me to him. If he had taken me there and then on the rug I don't think I would have resisted and everything, my own life and his, would have been very different. But as he laid me gently back on the rug and freed his prick from his trousers he made the mistake of asking my permission. "Please, Gertrude!" he said.

Something within me snapped. Why did he have to ask my permission if he was so sure of his ideas? Why did he not ram it home to the hilt in the budding lips of my cunt? I turned over quickly on to my belly. "Take me there if you wish," I said coldly, presenting my anus.

And he did. Poor, weak Harry did as he was told! How easy it would have been for him to raise me and ram it into my cunt from behind! But no! He laid his knob respectfully on my anus, and a moment later, with a little sigh of pain, I felt the thick shaft sink in between my buttocks.

He tried to hurt me then, consciously. He was taking his revenge upon me. Poor Harry! Had he forgotten that Pain was my element? That I lived in it as a fish in water or as a salamander in a flame?

When he came he collapsed, hiding his face in the back of my neck. I lay with my head turned towards the fire, staring at the dying embers.

๛

In the middle of the night someone was knocking on the door of my bedroom.

Was it Harry? Had he come to plead again?

"Go away!" I said. "I want to sleep!"

I heard voices.

Then Harry's voice said: "Please open up, Gertrude. It's urgent. Someone is here to see you."

I yawned. I was angry with Harry. He had almost convinced me and then he had given the lie to his own words by being afraid to act.

"Can it not wait until morning?"

"It can't, Gertrude."

I put on a black dressing gown, brushed my hair and applied lipstick heavily at the dressing table, and then, in a leisurely way, I opened the door.

Harry stood there and behind him, slightly in shadow, another man.

"You have an important visitor, my lady."

I looked behind him at the man who stood in shadow.

"You may go, Mr. Prentice," the man's voice said. His voice had a foreign intonation.

It was not until Harry had gone downstairs that the man stepped forward out of shadow.

I was struck at once by the whiteness of the skin under the close black beard and moustache, the prominent cheekbones which accentuated the great hollows from which two black eyes glittered commandingly. The stranger was tall, dressed impeccably in a suit of dark gray.

He bowed.

"May I enter, Madame?"

I stepped back to allow him to enter.

He surveyed the room at a glance and walked straight to the fireplace where he stood, his back towards me, one fine hand resting on the mantlepiece, gazing down at the flickering coals.

I closed the door quietly, locked it, and stood hesitantly near the bed. Who could he be? What on earth was his business at this time of night?

It was a moment before he spoke.

"I attended the meeting in the Temple tonight," he said simply. "I sat near the back."

"Oh, you are a Member?"

He turned to face me, his gaunt and handsome face betraying nothing.

"My name is Miguel Maria Hernandez de Cordoba. I am the Third Pain Cardinal."

I gasped. He couldn't have been more than thirty-five. I had imagined old men, twelve old men.

"I came about you, Gertrude, but not to see you. I came to see your Grand Painmaster. Where is Sir William?"

"In the cellar," I said nervously.

"What is he doing there?"

"He was in the front two rows. They are to be detained for a week's flagellation."

"And you have authority over your Grand Painmaster?"

"No, but he was corrupt. If you were there you saw that! His identity was known to Lord E. . ."

"So he was corrupt?"

"Yes!" I said, my voice tinged with defiance.

"And what is corruption, Gertrude?"

I didn't answer.

"And yet you were so fluent tonight when you spoke to the Members of order and hierarchy! I believe you implied that corruption was disorder, a lack of reverence for hierarchy. Is that not so? But Sir William is above you in the Hierarchy of the Order of Pain. Thus your action of depriving him of his liberty was corrupt. Do you understand?"

"But. . . "

"There are no 'buts' about it, Gertrude. You had no authority whatsoever to incarcerate your superior in the cellars. Send down and release him at once!"

I rang a bell.

Willie appeared at a small private door at the side.

"Go down and release Sir William," I said.

"Ask him to come up here," the Third Pain Cardinal added.

My visitor turned again to the fire.

He did not speak again until Sir William entered. When Sir William saw him, he fell on his knees before the Cardinal and kissed his hand.

"Eminence!" he said quietly.

The Cardinal gave the signal for him to rise.

"I ask you, Sir William, to pardon this headstrong young woman. She will no doubt ask your pardon herself in a more suitable place."

Sir William bowed. "Your wish is my command, Eminence!"

"Excellent. Then we can proceed," the Cardinal said. "I have come directly from the Seat itself," he continued, "to find out more about the young woman who is now one of us." He nodded towards me. "It is said in all official correspondence that she is still a virgin. Is that so?"

Sir William nodded. "To the best of my knowledge that is true, Eminence. I had Oakes's word on it."

"And what of your knowledge, Gertrude?" said the Cardinal to me with the suspicion of a smile.

"I am a virgin," I said dully, and as I said it I felt regret that I hadn't given myself to Harry. Why had the Cardinal not reprimanded Sir William for his treachery to the Order?

The Cardinal's lashes fell over his dark eyes almost imperceptibly, like the wing of a delicate insect.

He turned back to the other.

"Leave me with Gertrude now, Sir William. I shall call on you tomorrow afternoon at your home on some other business."

"Yes, Eminence."

Once again Sir William went to his knees, kissed the Cardinal's hand, and backed away. He left the room quietly.

"You are out of temper, Gertrude?"

I flashed a look that was meant to be contemptuous at him.

He smiled. It was a beautiful smile. "You think that I am corrupt because I didn't reproach Sir William? You are a foolish girl, Gertrude. Should I upbraid your superior in front of you?"

I hung my head.

When I looked up he was standing close to me, his face not a foot from my own. His eyes were kind and searching.

"Tell me, Gertrude, you are not easy in your mind; I want to know why."

I walked over to the fire and sat down on a stool.

"It's nothing really," I said. "It's just that there doesn't seem to be anything left. I feel as though I'll be bored for the rest of my life."

He sat down near me, his hand stroking the fine hairs of his beard near the cheek.

"Go on, Gertrude."

"There's no more to say," I said. "I thought it would give me pleasure to be Painmistress. It doesn't. All those foolish people having to be bullied to take their illicit pleasure. And what is there for me? Money? Power? These things don't interest me. I'm sick of the world! I nearly gave myself to Harry Prentice tonight, that's how bored I had become. And I would have, and still would even now if I hadn't known it would just be the same afterwards. Do you understand? Does no one understand?"

"I understand perfectly," the Cardinal said. "When I examined your dossier at the Holy Seat I suspected as much. *There is no future for you in the Order, Gertrude.* When I saw and heard you tonight my thoughts were confirmed. You are too zealously religious, too pure. For you, the logic of your terrible passion is inescapable. In the world, in the Congregation, there can only be repetition, anti-climax. That is not for you, Gertrude. But you cannot expect all these worldly people to accept your terrible logic. It is *your* destiny, not theirs."

As he spoke he had reached over and taken my hand.

"You know what I mean, Gertrude?"

He was staring into my eyes. In the depth of his eyes a holy fire seemed to burn. I was fascinated and frightened but above all glad, glad that someone else had looked into my heart and recognized the terrible passion that lurked there.

"Yes."

"And you accept it?"

"Yes."

"You will die naked, nailed to a cross, near the Holy Seat. You will die for us, and to affirm your own great passion, and your agony will be a light for us who are condemned to live on." He spoke as though he were hypnotized.

"Yes."

He got up and once again laid one of his beautiful hands on the mantlepiece. He stared at the fire.

"We have been waiting for you for a long time, Gertrude."

"When?"

"Not yet awhile, my child. Your sacrifice must coincide with some plans we have at the Seat and they are not yet mature." He looked at me keenly. "It may take five years, Gertrude."

"Oh God! Why?"

"I cannot divulge the innermost secrets of the Order, my child! But anyway, you will have to be groomed for your great moment. You will come to Spain. The Cardinals themselves will wish to have control of your instruction."

"When will I go to Spain?"

"The day after tomorrow, Gertrude. You will travel with me."

I fell on my knees in front of him.

"Oh, thank you! Thank you!"

"You have no need to thank me, Gertrude," he said quietly. "It is your destiny."

Kneeling at his feet I was suddenly radiantly happy. I looked up at him. "Whip me, Master!" I whispered huskily.

He smiled.

"A thin cane," he said. "Get one from your servant."

I rang the bell and told Willie to bring a supple cane. He nodded delightedly but I could see he was disappointed when I told him on his presenting it to me to leave us alone. However, he went.

"Take off your dressing gown."

I slipped it off and stood naked before him. He looked at me for a long time.

"You are very beautiful, Gertrude," he said at last. He touched the warm mould of my breasts with his long fingers and then allowed them to fall to the shapely flatness of my belly. "Beautiful," he said again. "The room is alive with you, Gertrude. Your naked flesh radiates a warmth, such a delicate odor." His fingers brushed my cunt, which quivered at his touch. He was smiling gently. "There is an art to inflicting pain, Gertrude. I have seen women thrashed by men with no more imagination than butchers, big brutes who depended upon the weight of the forearm, on the brutality of the flail itself. I have watched them strike again and again, bruising flesh and breaking bones. All that is not only unnecessary but stupidly destructive. I have seen a woman unfit to walk for a month and who, after that month, had lost all her poise, all the proudness of her carriage. No, that is not the way of the great artist. See, here is the instrument!" He held the thin cane at either extremity and bent it into a bow. "It is subtle; it will break no bones. I shall strike you three times, Gertrude, with science, with art. With those three strokes you will accomplish your agony. There is no need either to tire myself or to put you through a protracted pain. Some of your instruments are clumsy bonebreakers. I want you now to touch your toes. The first stroke is purely introductory, painful enough even though it is delivered on the fat part of the buttocks, but its object is to arouse the sweats of anticipation. After the first stroke you will do a back-bend, you know what that is? Your front is then exposed. When you are in that position, quivering from the pain of the first stroke, the other two strokes will be delivered almost together. The first will strike you across the breasts, just below the nipples. You will scream with the acutest agony and no doubt begin to collapse. But at once, before you have collapsed, I shall strike again, this time striking the soft underside of the mound itself, the clitoris, and of course upper thighs. There will be no need for more."

He was gazing at me gently.

"Are you ready, Gertrude?"

Without replying, my throat filled with lust and my eyes heavy with love for the man who was about to deliver the fatal caress, I dropped at the waist, my long hair falling towards the ground—I could already feel the sweat gathering at my temples—and thrust my haunted buttocks out eagerly as my hands groped for my feet . . .

The Lost Years

At this point there is a break in the narrative and in the following pages of the notebook there is no further reference to Gertrude Gault. By the time we meet her again it is December 1921 and the protagonist is called Carmencita de las Lunas.

Under this alias—she is now obviously twenty years of age and of striking beauty— she appears to have made a reputation for herself in the tradition of the Great Courtesans. She was seen often in the fashionable underworlds of both Madrid and Barcelona and always in the company of some rich nobleman or other. There can be no doubt that some of these noblemen belonged to the Order and that some, at least, among them were Pain Cardinals within it.

Of the characters whom we met in the first part of the narrative only two, apart from Carmencita herself, are carried over into the latter part. Miguel Maria Hernandez de Cordoba, whose object in making Gertrude wait five years seems to have been a purely selfish one, and Willie, the little Glasgow cobbler who seems to have gone with Gertrude to Spain as her body servant. There is, unfortunately, no more word of Harry Prentice, who came so near to saving Gertrude from her terrible fate, and in my subsequent inquiries in Glasgow I found no conclusive evidence in relation to him. There were three possible trails. One led to Indo-China, one to Australia, and the other to America. I was not in a position to undertake such an extensive search.

Nor did I ever find Hazel Cooper, although she was well-enough remembered in the Gorbals as Razor King's last mistress.

Of Miguel Maria Hernandez de Cordoba, I think it can be safely said that the man was mad. As far as I can make out—indeed, Carmencita says so herself, although she doesn't appear to hold it against him, was flattered rather—his sole object in delaying the crucifixion was to wait for his own elevation to the position of Pain. He himself, as Carmencita's somewhat incoherent narrative suggests, wished to drink of her last passion. We can picture the gaunt bearded face, its lustrous black eyes reflecting the moonlight, thrusting itself voraciously between the soft bleeding thighs of the dying woman, to suck there with his red lips the very slime of her dying. I have no doubt that that is precisely what happened, for the ambiguous Miguel was elected to the Holy Office in December, 1921. Two months later, his position established, he slaked his devilish thirst at the cross.

Of Willie there is little to be said. He seems to have been a loyal ministering angel right up to the last days, a humble shadow moving in the radiant twilight of this woman's mad dreams, always there to aid and abet her, and to dote on her pain-twisted body. There is no evidence that he was present at the crucifixion and I rather think he wasn't. I found no trace of him after the most extensive researches although I was able to locate the cobbler's shop where the two of them had indulged in their terrible lusts. It is no longer a cobbler's shop. The new tenant sells fish and chips.

ॐ

There is little point in further clarification. Gertrude's own narrative, although somewhat incoherent in form, is (if read sympathetically) straightforward enough. The years between have been lost. There is no reference to the journey to Spain nor to the intervening years up until 1921, no large reference that is to say, none anyway upon which we could hope to build a history. One last point worth mentioning before we present Gertrude's final narrative: Pasted in the notebook were a number of cuttings from newspapers of Madrid and Barcelona. They were all in the form of society gossip: "Prince B. . . was seen in the company of an unknown woman last night. It is hinted that she was Carmencita de las Lunas, an almost legendary queen of the underworld. She was heavily veiled . . . "

The Road to the Cross

*T*highs, mine, white, soft, and his tongue licking amongst the hair. "Suck it up!" I whispered, feeling wet now at the crotch and a trickle of sweat on my belly which still smarted from the cane. I thought I would burst open at the fourth stroke. His beard is soft and gentle and insinuating, like a cat, and I asked him again when it would happen and he said: "Soon now, little Carmen!" And I knew that he meant he was going to be Pain and that was why we had waited. And I could feel his head on my soft belly and his breathing amongst my thighs. Sometimes he stabbed his thumb into my cunt and my buttocks rose to meet the thrust. He is brutal then as though he would like to ram his way into my entrails. "You're bleeding," he said, and I was, it was my period, and he smeared the blood on my belly and on my thighs and under bedclothes. I had a breath of my own sweet-sickly smell and his male sweat. There is nothing about me he doesn't love! His little Carmen! It's funny how I am the only one who loves him. They say he is the hardest and cruelest of them all, like my father was! And his daughter, her sweat and pain is for nothing but his delight! Ah, Miguel! You alone will help me to die into ecstasy! My only love! My dark murderer! "Suck me now. I am tired! My flesh is so tired! Suck me all away!"

And Willie sneaked Prince B . . . into my bedchamber! I was actually rubbing myself in front of the mirror when he stepped from behind the curtains!

Carmencita! That is what he called me! I informed him that we had never formally been introduced. I had seen him, of course, about the town and I had heard of his lust for me. Oh, he didn't hide that! A rope of pearls, diamond clips. M. le Comte de Z . . . came to see me. An emissary. His Royal Highness would gladly ruin himself! I should ask, and it would be granted to me! "Ask the prince if he loves me enough to strike a knife to my heart!" The gentleman paled. He was certain the prince would sooner thrust a dagger in his own. "How very selfish of him!" I replied. "Ah, my Lady, you do him a grave injustice!" "Justice, sir? Let him do justice to all the hot little bitches that surround him! Your sister for example!" He would have struck me, so I struck him first, and then he couldn't strike back for he was a gentleman! "Get out of here, sir, and tell the prince, your master, that if he has anything to say to me he had better come himself. I want none of his dogs around here!"

Ha! How I laughed when he had gone, poor M. le Comte de Z . . .

My belly was very white in the mirror with its chevron of black hair at the mound and two thin red lines, cane-marks which had not yet disappeared. I bent slightly at the knees and inserted my finger gently into my cunt. And it was at that moment that Prince B. . . stepped from behind the curtains.

"Forgive me, Carmencita!" He went down on his knees before me.

"I do not know you, sir! No one has introduced us! How dare you hide in my bedroom!"

"Forgive me!"

I smiled to see him kneel there.

I wriggled my bare hips provocatively and sidled forward until my cunt was a foot from his face.

He looked up at me with his pale face.

"Kiss it!" I commanded.

He did so passionately. I forced him away.

"And now, get out!" I said.

"No, please! Carmencita, please!"

"How dare you, sir! Do you expect me to allow you to fuck me on the spot? Just because you've had the bad manners to break into my bedroom unannounced?"

My vulgarity pained him. This was not what he had expected of his Venus.

"Let me kiss your hand!" he implored.

"Sir, you have just kissed my cunt! Let us please avoid bathos! Stand up now!"

He stood up like a soldier springing to attention. I moved against him and put my arms around his neck. I looked into his eyes and brought his lips down against mine. He held me tightly in his arms, his hands impressing themselves in the soft flesh of my back.

"Do you love my body more than God?" I whispered.

"Yes! Oh yes, Carmencita!"

"You will obey me?"

"Anything, my darling!"

"Whip me, Prince!" I looked derisively into his eyes, which registered shock and incomprehension. I pointed to a thin cane which lay on my bed. "Take it up and whip me!" I commanded. He moved over to the bed like a sleepwalker. "Test it!" I said. "Test it in the air as though you meant it!"

He did so with a mixture of fascination and horror in his eyes.

"Good."

I bent down in front of him, presenting the smooth cream of my buttocks. "Three strokes, Prince! Come, show me you're a man!"

He moved then and gave me three sharp cuts on the buttocks. Only the third was half hearted. Immediately afterwards he broke the cane and threw himself apologetically on my buttocks, kissing the marks. "Oh, forgive me, Carmencita!"

I moved nimbly away from him.

"What a ninny you are, Prince! And you expect me to love you! Why, you don't want to be my master, you want to be my slave! Well then, my slave you shall be!"

I laughed at him.

"Come, I shall dress now and you will take me to a fine restaurant. Is that what you want?"

"Oh yes, Carmencita! Anything! Ask anything!"

"Perhaps I will, but meanwhile I shall dress!"

As his carriage brought me to my door again he pleaded to be allowed to spend the night with me. "You want to make love to me?" He smothered my gloved

hands with kisses. "Kill me first then, Prince, and make
love to my body. My warm body will not resist you!"

He shook his head sadly, without comprehension.

"Then goodnight, Prince! When you come, bring your
knife with you!"

ॐ

In the darkness of my room I lie awake. My hands cup
my breasts. My naked legs stretch far apart and the soft
sheet falls against my mound. How many men muttering hoarsely in the night have worshiped there with
their lips, with their hands, feasting their eyes, and been
powerless to bring their own loins in sacred contact.
No, my beautiful male! Give me it in my lips but do not
do that.

I see my dead father and the women sprawling in the
slums, white puttylike flesh quivering, animals, their big
thighs stung into heat and hot fear by his rampant prick.
And I lie alone, and everything has receded into the
familiar sound of my own breathing. I am left only with
my awareness of it. And then, gradually I come into
another world, a close and confederate consciousness of
my own softness and the sound of my breathing and
nothing more and there is nothing to which I am related.
And now I come to know that it is my body which is soft,
the thighs, my little belly, set and smooth as a watchglass
on a fine watch, and that it is I and not my body which is
aware. And now I am conscious of existing and being
alone. And I cannot be conscious of myself as existing
without at the same time being conscious of myself as

135
ॐ

existing alone and in relation to instants in time and points in space which hold themselves off from me and which escape me, for I have not the power to draw them back to myself out of my memory. And the room comes back with its dark corners, and the fire flickering and the paler gray panel of the open window, and night sounds, and now I know myself to be wide awake and alone. Spain, and the time is drawing near. In Spain everything is red and black and the color of a dancer's thighs as she twirls and snaps her heels as though shuffling her cunt for her mate. Spanish women have splendid haunches and big rubbery teats. They grow fat quickly. They are sexually strong.

I spread my arms out and my legs and I already feel the heavy nails which will rivet my hands and feet to receive Pain. Can no man's hand excite me now? Must it always be the thongs? I call Willie. I am unable to sleep. He is there like a shadow at my bedside, holding a candle. "Willie, I'm dying of waiting! Take me somewhere! I must have violence done!"

And then I am heavily veiled and Willie guides me through narrow streets. Hovels. A stench of oil and wine. Tipsy voice. "In here, my Lady!"

We step over a sleeping cur. A fat woman feeding a baby at one large blob of breast. She has three gold teeth and her pregnant belly lies like a sack of flour on her knees. She looks after us. "Up here!"

We climb up dingy stone stairs inside a patio. He flings open a door which emits a cloud of blue smoke and coarse laughter. We are in a brothel. The women leer at me as Willie guides me to a table in the corner. Wine. The room is full of sailors and big-breasted women with unkempt hair. Some sailors are watching me. I quiver with anticipation. I am heavily veiled.

Willie whispers to the waiter, a dwarf with one leg, the other a pegleg. The waiter winks. He leers at me. He goes away.

"Drink some wine."

There is too much noise to speak. A sailor has twisted a woman backwards so that her big meaty breasts are naked and is dousing them with red wine. She is screaming, kicking, her fat thighs gartered with green silk. Someone knocks over a chair. A blind guitarist is playing flamenco. They are clapping their hands. A drunken prostitute lurches over to me and tries to rip the veil from my face. Willie catches her by the hair and throws her to the ground. Two sailors are going to deal with Willie but the pegleg comes back and tells them to fuck off. For some reason or other they obey him. He whispers to Willie and winks. Willie nods. He beckons me to stand up. We pass through a bead curtain and go up another flight of stairs. We are in an attic with a wooden floor and only a bed-frame strung with wire. Pegleg brings in two stools. Two fat women come in, strip naked, and begin to rub their bellies together. They grunt. One of them farts. The other one laughs hoarsely with a flash of gold teeth. They grin at us and lie on the floor, each with her head between the other's legs. They snort like pigs and roll over, tonguing each other, their big white buttocks gathering dust from the floor. They smell. Pegleg stands guard at the door, his arms folded across the little barrel of a chest, and grins. One woman is now making water over the other's thigh. The splashed one is giggling deliriously. They get up on their big fleshy feet. They look at me and approach. Willie moves off to the side. I look after him fearfully. What is going to happen? And then they are on me. One rips off my veil and the other, throwing me to the floor, begins to tear the clothes off my body. I am bruised and half naked. I struggle. The bigger of the two women clamps my head between her thighs and holds me to the ground. This is the first time I have tasted another woman's sex. The bristling hairs rub my mouth until it opens. It tastes foul, of piss and sweat. I am nearly suffocated. I am pinioned to the floor. I buck with my buttocks and legs. The spin of my buttocks is grazed as I am forced suddenly and painfully to the floor as the weight of the second woman falls on my thighs. Her mouth is at my sex and her big slobbering tongue is already working my clitoris. I begin to enjoy the violence and I struggle ferociously. The more I struggle the harder they clamp me down. My belly is scratched. I scream. Laughter. Suddenly they are both up and they are kicking me with their hard feet. I rise to my knees and my head is jammed against the other woman's cunt. The same sour taste. It slips softly like a jellyfish about my face, containing my nose and mouth. The other helps to pinion me in that position while she slaps my buttocks with her hand. I am thrown to the floor again. I find myself momentarily free. I stand up and back against the far wall. They stand with their hands on their naked hips, laughing, their bellies thrust out and tufted with coarse hair. They come towards me together. I cringe. A needle of anticipation moves somewhere deep in my belly. And now they start slapping me methodically and I spin drunkenly about between them, reeling against their solid flesh, pushed and slapped until I fall painfully across the iron bedstead. I have fallen on my front, and one of my breasts has gone between the wires, which cut painfully. A knee is jammed in the small of my back and they are tying me to the bedframe, a foot or a hand at each corner. I struggle but it is of no use. My face cranes around. Pegleg is standing close, his cock out in his hand. He brings it near my face and shakes it. It is an enormous prick for a four-foot dwarf. He brings it close to my lips. I don't try to turn my head away. I allow it to lie lightly against them. My tongue moves out slowly and I lick the tip. It too tastes of urine. I move my nostrils against it and sniff softly. Who told me it was bad? The odor excites me. He is leering at me. Suddenly someone has struck me hard across the buttocks with a slat of wood. My forehead falls against the wires. I forget the prick. I reach only for the pain, and it comes again, even more brutally. I breathe heavily. My body perspires freely. I allow it to droop against the crisscross wires of the bedstead.

Suddenly there is laughter, male laughter, drunken. I realize that half a dozen sailors have been allowed into the room. Someone is rubbing grease on my anus. I wiggle it frantically against the rubbing fingers. Someone says: "She's hot for it now. Who's first?" A male front pinions me to the bed. A cocktip is laid against my anus. Pressure is increased. It slides in its whole length painfully. "Buggered her!" someone shouts. "Ride her!" yells another. The big member is going in and out like a piston and the man is sweating freely. "Fuck you! Fuck you!" he is grunting. His teeth sink into the back of my neck. "Bite the hot bitch!" someone shouts. I whinny with pleasure, like a struck mare, the stallion mounted. Nothing now but the pleasant pain and the strange feeling of penetration within my vitals.

No sooner has the first man ejaculated and rolled off than the second, hot, dry, and excited, lands on my sweating buttocks and strikes home like a well-aimed poker. The torment at my bowels is growing. The crisscross wires of the bedstead cut into my soft front as it is jerked about under the violent male movement. "Jesus!" the man is muttering as he slobbers in my ear, "Jesus! Jesus!" I begin to groan with pain. "She's coming! She's coming!" a voice is urging enthusiastically through the mists of pain and sweat. The man on top shudders violently and bucks like a bronco-rider into satisfaction.

"Turn her over! She's got a cunt, hasn't she?" a new voice cries.

Willie's voice rises in protest. I hear a thud. Someone has struck him. A moment later I am unbound and dragged to the floor on my back. I struggle and protest through sweat and tears but my thighs are forced apart at the knees and a hard cock thrusts its way easily into my juicy cunt. It is like dying. Into my consciousness comes the thought that I am no longer a virgin. What has happened? What have I allowed to be done! But I have no time for further thought. The man is coming. "What a cunt! what a cunt! what a fucking juicy cunt!" he is grunting as he rises like a springboard in his ecstasy and descends on me, belly to belly, to loose his flood of sperm. "Me next!" a voice cries, and it has a familiar ring. A moment later I become aware of the grinning head of Pegleg, the dwarf, at the level of my breasts. His big cock has already sunk into me and soon he is nibbling cruelly at my left nipple. A black cock is thrust into my mouth suddenly, for Pegleg, being too short, has left that vacant. I close my eyes and submit willingly to every humiliation, and soon, in spite of the general pain, a deep sense of peace comes over me. *Use me as you will!* All of you! All of you! I can think of nothing else. My flesh is only for sacrifice. In that sacrifice is my peace . . .

৯৫

How many days before Miguel found me?

He found me in the brothel, stark naked, in a filthy condition, reeling drunkenly amongst the sailors, those wonderful ruffians! I was confined to the attic room. A few tables had been brought in so that sailors could drink there, spending money as they played with me. And how they played! It was strange that it hadn't occurred to me before, this thought that I might find my peace in a brothel. They played with me as though I was a thing. They slapped me, fucked me, buggered me, passing me amongst them like a ball. One of their favorite games was to make me act like a bitch in heat. I was made to go around on all fours, scratching myself and sniffing their chairlegs. One of them, his glass of red wine balanced high, would whip out his prick and make me sniff that and lick it. At the same time they made me shake my but-tocks as though I were wagging my tail.

And how I wagged my little tail!

I wagged it so well, my little hot buttocks quivering, and the tuft of my cunt, wet usually, for they made me pee by raising my leg just like a little bitch dog, really like a stringy little tail jutting between my legs, yes, I wagged it so well they used to get down on their knees and sniff along after me. Woof-woof! Woof-woof! And when that happened I would raise my buttocks by sinking forward on to my forearms, and sluck! A big cock would be in from the back, right in my quivering cunt! Ooooh! And then they would clap their hands in time to our quivering jube-jube movement. Ride-the-hot-bitch, ride-the-hot-bitch, ride-the-hot-bitch! And his last jolt would slap me forward on to the floorboards with my belly and breasts. As often as not they would pour a glass of wine over me before the next one slapped it into me.

And one night I had a good idea. I always wanted to stir up violence in them. I was making my rounds, sniffing chairlegs and ankles as usual, and they were all just beginning to get bawdy and to describe to one another just what they were going to do with me, this back and forth across the tables in the midst of drinking and laughter. Well, suddenly I cocked up my little leg and winkled on a sailor's foot. The whole room roared with laughter. The sailor upon whom I had pissed stared for a moment as though he didn't understand and then he threw back his chair with a loud crash and booted me hard on the soft underbelly so that I went sprawling on my back across the floor. "Ya filthy little bitch! Pee on me, would ya!" He leapt after me, grasping his prick from his fly as he did so, and it was hard as a bone, and he fucked me in the cunt there and then. And that night was wonderful and they did everything but kill me until the early hours of the morning.

One day Willie came. He looked worried and said that Miguel was looking for me and had threatened to kill him if he didn't find me. There had been a quarrel. Miguel suspected Prince B. . . of having spirited me off. Prince B. . . accused Miguel of having corrupted me. And it had ended in a duel. No one was killed, but Prince B. . . received a bullet wound in the shoulder and was still confined to bed. And it wasn't only Miguel who had contacted Willie. Prince B. . . had asked Willie to visit him and offered him the equivalent of a thousand pounds if he would conduct him to me. Willie didn't know what to do.

I told him to take the money and to conduct Prince B. . . to my kennel one night, any night when the sailors were there.

I was in the middle of my turn when he arrived, as pale as death, and leaning heavily on a stick. When I saw him standing in the doorway I put out my tongue as a dog does and breathed quickly, like a happy bitch. He stared at me for more than a minute during which I turned my buttocks towards him and wagged my tail. That caused the sailors who had been silent since he entered to burst out again into drunken laughter. One of them got on to his knees and began to sniff me, and in that way he chased me amidst loud laughter in circles around the floor. My last sight of Prince B. . . was his almost collapsing against the door frame and then suddenly he was gone. That made the sailors even more fun. They fucked me and stuck me and made a fine mess of me that night. Willie joined in and began to show them how to use a cane.

After that I got a sound whipping every night until my bottom was red and black and blue.

Prince B. . . must have informed Miguel of my whereabouts. Perhaps he suggested that Miguel was the only one who could get me away. And that was true. And that was what happened.

Miguel came.

I had been wagging my little tail and a sailor was standing on a chair with his cock out and I was pretending to be begging for it as a dog does, and at that moment I saw Miguel standing in the doorway. I froze at once and stared at him. He simply nodded for me to follow him and I did. I walked right out of my wonderful life at the brothel into a carriage which took me to a country estate. There Miguel chained me naked to a wall and beat me within an inch of death.

ॐ

ॐ

When I finally came to consciousness next day I was in bed. He must have been sitting waiting. He was, as usual, impeccably dressed and he looked very severe.

He spoke at once when he knew I was awake.

"You are no longer a virgin."

"No."

"You are simply a prostitute."

"Yes."

"A sailor's whore."

"Yes."

"A cunt!"

"Yes."

"And what do you expect me to do now?"

"Send me back to the brothel," I said in a tired voice. "I was happy there."

"You were happy. Have you forgotten Pain?"

"No. I didn't intend it to happen. First I was raped. I liked it. Then it didn't matter. What else could I do?"

"You should have come back at once before you were seen by Prince B . . ."

"What difference does it make?"

"It makes a great deal of difference."

I shook my head without comprehension.

"Do you not understand," he said, leaning forward and speaking in an intense voice, "that I will allow nothing, *nothing,* to stand in the way of your crucifixion?"

I shook my head hopelessly.

"I am no longer a virgin, Miguel."

"But if only you and I know it? That is why Prince B . . . should never have known!"

"Does it make no difference to you?"

"Not a whit!"

"But why? How could I become the Virgin Death?"

"I told you once, my dear, that you were too pure for us, the worldly people. I am interested in the Order in the world. Last night, in secret conclave, I was elected. I became Pain. Nothing now stands in the way of the crucifixion. Nothing, that is, except your stupidity."

"We waited too long, Miguel. You should have crucified me years ago."

"That was not possible before I became Pain."

"Why not? Are you the only one in the Order who wishes a Virgin Death?"

"Not at all, my dear. But, from the beginning, I decided that I and I alone would drink of it. And it is the privilege of Pain, of no other."

"And that's why you kept me waiting?" I studied him. "I would have liked you to be the one to drink, Miguel." I closed my eyes. "So I was right? The Order is corrupt from top to bottom."

"Corrupt? What is that? Everything is relative, my beloved Carmen, except death. Death alone is absolute and that is why you, the purest of us, lust after it."

"Someone else said that, that everything was relative. Do you remember Harry Prentice?"

"The man was no diplomat. He lost you."

"And you are, and you didn't?"

"That is correct. But for this one slip, this foolishness of letting Prince B. . . know that you had become a sailor's whore, everything would have been straightforward."

"What about the sailors, the dwarf, the other whores? They saw me fucked too."

"They are not important. They had no idea who you were. For them you were simply an amusing lady who had become a nymphomaniac. It is Carmencita de las Lunas who matters, and everyone knows that she has never known a man. Why do you think you are the most famous courtesan in Madrid? Simply because you are unobtainable."

"Prince B. . . knows."

"Yes, Prince B. . . knows, but of course he has told no one, not even his closest acquaintances. You, he, and myself possess the secret. You will die without revealing it on the cross. I will be Pain magnified by the last passion of the Virgin. As for B. . ., I first thought of killing him. I am very sorry I did not aim to kill in the duel. But at the time there was no necessity for it. It was a stupid affair of honor. But to murder him or even to challenge him to a second duel would be dangerous. He is an important man, and in a duel he might well betray our secret in his last words. I could not be sure of killing him outright at twenty paces. And anyway, we have both been warned. Dueling is not popular with the Court. No, that is why I have evolved a better idea . . . "

"What is that?"

"We have a great advantage. B. . . is madly in love with you. Thus he is capable of being bribed."

"How?"

"With you, little Carmen."

He got up and stood by the fireplace in his usual posture. He looked across at me, his eyes flickering.

"I intend to make Prince B. . . a proposal," he said. "I will offer him you as a doting mistress, to do as he will, until the night of the full moon in February, at which time he must surrender you to me and to your sacrifice. In return for these idyllic weeks I will pledge him to eternal silence. He will agree because he loves you and is very near to suicide and he will keep his word because he is a gentleman. So you see, little Carmen, all is not lost."

Two days later, in the early afternoon, Miguel returned.

"He is coming at four. This estate will be the place of your honeymoon. On no account must you leave it. You will be for him what he wishes you to be, gentle as a dove, vicious as a reptile, sensual as a geisha. You will obey him in everything within the boundaries of the estate until 7 P.M. on the night of the full moon. I shall come personally to fetch you."

He looked at his watch

"It is two o'clock," he said. "In a few minutes a number of gentlemen are coming up to see you. For them you are Carmencita, the Virgin. You must not speak of the prince, nor of your experience in the brothel."

I nodded.

I was dressed in scarlet silk which flowed to the floor like fiery liquid below my naked breasts. My nipples as usual were tinted black and my eyes elongated in a slant with mascara.

"You are very beautiful, Carmencita!"

He rang a bell and waited by the fireplace. I lay at length on a lemon-colored divan.

A moment later there was a discreet knock on the door. "Come in!"

Five gentlemen of varying ages entered the room. They bowed solemnly first to Miguel and then turned towards me. I rose off my divan to meet them. In turn, bowing low, they kissed my hand. They were all between forty and sixty and I could see they all found it difficult to keep their eyes off my breasts.

"Well, gentlemen?" Miguel said from the fireplace. "I think no one can accuse me of exaggerating, eh?"

The gentlemen nodded gravely. The eldest of them, a man with white hair and a small Van Dyke beard, said: "May I question our Lady?"

Miguel nodded.

"Of course, gentlemen. She is at your disposal."

"Are you a virgin?" the man with the white beard asked.

"Yes," I said, and as soon as I said it, it occurred to me that I could have chosen not to and that in choosing to say it I had signed my death warrant.

"You are certain you have never been penetrated in the normal way by a male penis?"

"I am certain, sir."

"And you know what our Order plans for you?"

"I know."

"And you accept?"

"I demand!" I replied. I noticed a fleeting smile on Miguel's face.

The old gentleman was slightly put out. He hemmed and hawed. But finally he said he had no more questions.

"And you, gentlemen?" Miguel said to the others.

"No questions," the others said.

"Very well," Miguel said. "It is my intention now that she should remain here on this estate until the night. She will not be allowed to leave and she will practice meditation in preparation for her great trial. During this time she will not be disturbed by us. I myself shall pay her a weekly visit. Simply to see that she has all she requires. And now gentlemen, you may bestow the kiss."

He turned to me, pointing towards my thighs. "Carmen, if you please."

I guessed at once what was wanted. I opened the dress at the front to expose my cunt, tossed my head so that my long black hair fell on to my naked shoulders.

One by one the gentlemen went on their knees in front of me and applied their lips to my hot sex. The occasion seemed to be solemn so I didn't move. Each as he rose to his feet bowed and stepped aside. When they had all delivered their kiss they turned at once and left.

When they were gone, Miguel spoke:

"Now I myself will take my leave. I will not pay you a weekly visit. I will not see you again until I come to fetch you for your last passion. When I leave this house now you are the mistress of this estate and Prince B. . . is your adored lover. In case you have anything to communicate to me you may contact me through the tall footman called Angelo."

"Have you anything else to say to me, Miguel?"

"Nothing."

"You don't want to make love to me . . . once?"

He paused. Finally he said: "No, Carmen. I want more than that of you, and I shall have it at the Cross. Who knows if I took that from you now would I have the courage to take the other then?"

He smiled and left the room.

I was alone, waiting for my lover.

The Honeymoon

I am thinking all the time of these weeks now, the only weeks of ordinary love I have ever known. Night after night of sensuality. And the days.

When he came into the room I was lying on the divan. I was still wearing the red dress long and loose like a curtain which stopped, surprisingly, below my beautifully poised breasts. My nipples were still black, a jet, deep black which heightened enormously the sensual line of the breasts. I had brushed my straight black hair which fell just below the shoulders and I had given a letterbox look to my mouth with red paint.

He stood for a while just staring at me, as though I had stepped out of the sky, and then, crossing the room quickly, he threw himself to the floor beside the divan and showered my hands with kisses. I lifted his face across the line of my breasts close to my own and held us at a distance of six inches for a few moments until slowly and sensually I dragged his lips down against mine. At first I allowed them barely to touch. Sensing his growing passion I allowed my lips to collapse with a little inward take of breath and his tongue entered gently into my mouth's warm cave. He kissed me for a long time after he put his right hand to my left breast, then he lowered his lips and took the nipple in his mouth.

"You will keep our bargain?" I whispered.

He didn't answer. His whole soul was adoring my breast. I didn't interrupt him. There was plenty of time. I would find out in that time just what he most urgently required of me. It would be his. I would stop at nothing, even, if he saw fit, I would accept death. The thought made the future more exciting. Yes, if Prince B. . . had the courage to be my murderer I would gladly give myself up to him. Not for his sake, for at the beginning I had hardly more than a vague sympathy for him, but simply to accomplish dying and to outwit Miguel. Not that I hated Miguel. I didn't. But he had, for purely selfish reasons, deceived me for over five years. Was I flattered? Perhaps. But why shouldn't I deceive him.

But Prince B. . . was so much like a child in his sucking my breast, or like an adult's version of a child, for a child is often more brutal. I lifted a child in Barcelona one day and gave it my breast. There was no milk and the child put all his puny little strength into sucking.

No. I didn't believe he would ever have the power to kill me. Would he, when he lost me, have the power to kill himself? It struck me as strange that I would never know the answer to that question.

He was looking at me passionately in the face.

"Carmencita!" he breathed.

I smiled adoringly at him.

He buried his face in my neck. What a child! Should I mother him? Is that what he really desires?

I thought not.

"Suck my cunt!" I said in a vicious whisper. "Come up under my dress, slowly, like a dog!"

When he hesitated with a defensive look of astonishment on his face I said intensely, putting lust in my throat: "Do it, my darling! That is what you want to do. Approach gradually with your lips and nose. Come! See if it is dangerous!"

I whirled my full skirt over his head.

With the shame of his face hidden I pushed his head down gently to the level of the divan, to the level of my calves, to the level of my knees. The skirt ballooned over him, his tent of lust.

"Listen!" I said urgently to him, in a soft but breathless and confederate voice: "Do what you want to do! You want to get used to the dark, you don't want to move yet. Don't run home to my cunt like a scared rabbit. Smell it out first! See that it is not dangerous first, that you're stronger than it, and then you can take it like a vandal! . . . But not now! Not yet! For you're not a vandal yet. You are only a mole. With a long snout, timorous, blind, you are not sure of what is ahead! It's like being under the sea. It is dark. It has an odor. Deep in this warm tropical sea there is a cave. In shadow. Go with suspicion. There is an octopus in the cave, a great sucking creature, a night. Let your tongue lie on your lower nostrils. Pant, but in a muffled way. You don't want the creature to hear. Sniff. Do you smell it? That's it. That. Slowly now with your nose and tongue smell my left knee cap. Drop a little saliva off. Lick it up. Taste it. Savor it. Now, slide your head round so that your nose and tongue touch the soft inside of my right knee. Wait. What's that? It's not it. It's something else. Warm. Overpowering. It smells like shit. Yes. It is the smell of shit. It is strange and interesting that smell of shit. No reason for panic there, now, move your nose up suddenly to smell my cunt, but from a distance, from between my knees, and then bare your teeth; smell through the teeth, salivate, get that wind on your palate. Now, tongue like a little prod ahead, explore the white vastness of my thighs. Dawn is breaking, see. I am lifting my skirt slightly. But not yet, gradually. Stop. You felt a hair at the tip of your nose, a long hair, a hair with an odor; you are near, very near. The tongue. Gently and dripping saliva let it go forward through your lips. Hold your breath. You feel the hairs at the tip of your tongue? Take a deep breath. A deep smell. Let a noise begin at the back of your throat, a hushed grunt. See, dawn is breaking. Stick your tongue out and lay it with its delicate tastebuds on the sweaty mat of hair. The cave is moving like a sponge, gently, suppurating, in the tide. The round bowls of the sea's bottom are lifting to your cheeks. It is light. Make a first tentative dent in the hairy mat. See it break red. It is a maw! It is a woman's cunt!"

I shuddered as his mouth thrust itself wetly amongst the hair. I farted softly and gripped his cheeks between my thighs in a soft vise. There, his tongue was in exploring the slimy pit beneath the mat of hair, tipping over the rubbery parts and sliding voluptuously in the great slime-trickle that moved down like a sap from the dark depths of my belly.

"Suck me dry!" I whispered. "Suck my big hairy slime-pit dry!"

His whole mouth burst into me, the hairs on his upper lip mingling with my cunt hairs.

When he had explored and sucked for about ten minutes I moved away suddenly, stood up and pulled my dress about my naked loins.

"That's enough for the moment, darling. We must talk a little. I shall ring for tea."

He gazed at me with fascination. He said nothing.

࿐

After tea we sat together on the divan. I allowed him to put his hand under my dress between my naked thighs. I began to caress his ear with my mouth. His fingers were at the thatch and he was parting the stickily dried hairs.

"Take my dress off," I said huskily. "I want you to kiss my belly and my breasts."

He didn't move quickly this time. Gently he undid the hooks at my ribs and slid the robe off my body like a soft sheath. I lay naked, my legs together, relaxed. I breathed deeply, distending my creamy belly provocatively.

"Your lips," I said. "Explore the surfaces. Your nose, smell me all over. The navel, under the breasts, the armpits. Yes, your lips amongst the hair under my left arm. Another little nest of corruption for you to explore . . ."

His tongue moistened and curled the hair into wisps under my armpits. His lips sucked and tugged at my nipples, lingered at my navel.

"Grunt and sniff!" I whispered huskily. "See how it rises towards your mouth. It's there. Taste it again."

This time he buried his head thoroughly in the pit of lust at my thighs and I spread him round with all my hot corruption.

"Your cock, take it out now . . . no, don't undress, not this time, it's not safe! Just your balls and cock. Stand up and waggle it for me. Make it really big! Yes, you wonderful big prick!"

It rose like a peg, pink and shiny where the foreskin slipped back.

"Waggle it. Tell him about the big hot cunt that's waiting for him . . . Now, kneel at my feet and start licking upwards from between the toes until your big stiff prick is between my knees."

His balls slipped up between my shins until I had his cock at its base between my knees. I gripped it tightly so that the tip was embedded between the soft slats of my thighs.

"Give yourself!" I whispered urgently and his first hot emission shot forth between my thighs and clung between the two surfaces in a curtain of slime.

He groaned and shuddered violently.

"Get up!" I said in a vulgar voice. "Get out of here and come back when you're ready to fuck!"

༄

When I heard him about to come back I pulled the wide silk bag down over my head and shoulders as far as my waist and held it on the inside with my hands tight upon my hip bones. Thus, kicking and grunting on the bed as he entered, I presented the aspect of the naked lower half of a woman protruding violently from a large scarlet pod.

It took him at least ten seconds to reach the divan where I bucked about violently with my hairy mound in the air.

"Carmencita!"

I grunted like a pig, my naked legs flailing about. He didn't speak again. He came at me, a beast of prey who had found a helpless and kicking victim in the forest. I felt myself grasped at the knees by strong fingers. They were forced apart and the weight of his front fell heavily between my thighs. He wasn't going to make any mistake this time. He intended to have me with his prick to its hilt in my cunt. I didn't fight him seriously. The fine muscles of my lower torso rippled under him until I felt the big prick sink in. It reminded me of the launching of a ship. The tip was placed, a little pressure exerted, and then . . . slooosh! as the hull cuts evenly into the water. Sunk in my cunt now, he flattened my legs under his, twisting his own sinewy ones around mine like creepers, riveting me to the bed. And then I felt him work at the bag. He intended to have me and not the anonymous cunt that hung down like a half-unwrapped lollipop. I relaxed entirely under him and when he slid the bag first over my belly and then on upwards over my swelling breasts I made no effort to hinder him. I breathed deeply as though he had overpowered me, as though now his eyes stared into mine I was truly his, and my eyes said so and the twitch of my nostrils and my wet red lips.

He was lying on top of me now with his whole body, his cock still sunk in me at my vital center, our legs entwined, our bellies met, my breasts securely within his

157

hollowed shoulders, and our mouths feeding on each other, gently.

The movement came slowly, like an earthquake gathering its power in the earth's bowels, a slight stiffening at the thighs answered at mine by a softening, by a concurrence of the soft flesh. His member slid tentatively out and in, just once. As though to echo, then, my buttocks moved, just a tremor, but it made the sweatpad of my belly vibrate against his and showed him I was ready for despoiling

"Now!" I whispered, rubbing my soft neck against his chin.

Ram. To the hilt. And then up like a fish spraying water and down into the deep! His movements began furtively and were answered with furtive consent. They continued with increasing violence, our bellies together, my mound nozzling like a great black bull trying to push down a fence, and my cunt stuck and struck, a prickfuck.

Again he didn't take long to come, a few moments of frenzied passion and his semen leapt boiling from his groin. I received him with a moan, as though he had touched me at my inmost nerve. And then I held him, my belly slithering and shuddering against his, until my cunt sucked the last drop from his prick. It was becoming dark. I covered us with a counterpane of silk. I took his head on my breast and we slept.

I was awakened by exploring hands.

The lips fitted round my nipples like a vice and the small sensating bead was sucked inwards and stretched.

158
স্

My thighs twitched and a controlling finger took me like a hook. Meat on a hook. The image stuck with me and I groaned and slid my belly against his.

We had sweated. The weather was cold, but unlike most rooms in Spain the rooms of this villa were well heated.

"Fuck me, darling!" I whispered in the darkness. "Fuck me to death!"

His cock was in again, hard, greasy, and his hot hairs packed in mine.

A delicious hot sensation of well-being grew at my loins as his vibrating strokes increased. It seemed to be endless, the pushing and the sliding and the slime.

He muttered something as he came, quivering as the strength left him, and he fell asleep at once in my arms.

I lay awake in the darkness, wondering at the tender passion this gentle lover inspired in me. Was my life a mistake? Was it here in these doting arms that I was intended by nature to find fulfillment?

What if he made me pregnant with all this doting love? How could he help doing so?

We had not yet spoken of the pledge. Would he keep it? Certainly not if I was against it, if I asked him to take me away to safety and to love.

I almost convinced myself.

But how foolish of me! How could this passion last? What if I bore his child? Gradually the fire would turn to cinders and he would look about speculatively at other women. And then would I take a lover? Or more than one?

Futility. Life held nothing more for me than anticlimax. To be raised periodically to a high level of passion and then to sink once more, to the depths. My body suddenly sickened of this cloying love. Gradually, like a shadow in my blood, moved the absolute knowledge of the thongs.

Thongs.

Thongs.

Thongs.

What was this soft, docile beast lying at my side, simulating rape according to rite and instruction. Do this. Do that.

With no sting of the real.

With no butcher's red hands.

Imagine hands. Broad and thick. The nails clogged with blood. Of other victims.

Imagine a woman's white belly, its soft blotting-paper finish. The black cunt. And glimmering underneath, red, like a centipede. Soft lover, you forget history, and the claw.

I was staring up into darkness at the ceiling above. The man beside me no longer existed. He was void. A civilized creature.

Oh Miguel! After this sickly hell the gore and triumph of the cross!

Come! Live in the present. Many weeks till the cross. This man who sleeps at your side like a great tame brute, excite him, strike him to the quick, make him turn; perhaps yet he will have a readiness to do murder . . .

"My darling!" I whispered. "Wake up! Your Carmencita wants to speak to you!" I sensed his eyes flicker.

"Carmencita!"

"Il toro . . . " I whispered.

In Spain the man dies in agony in the form of the bull. The woman with her subtle changes of tone, the flirt, the repulser of advances, the one who piques, the one who controls and kills. It is all there in the bullring, in the sun of the late afternoon. The romantic passion, the striving after the absolute, tends towards death. That is the passion of the decadent Spanish men, the lovers, sadness, ecstasy, tragedy.

"Il toro . . . "

And this man beside me was a Spaniard. For all his youth he is old. He is tired. He wants to be mastered and tamed. He wants to be taught to accept death. Kill me now, quickly, you have flirted extravagantly with the cape when I was most wild, you have repulsed me with the horses and the pike to show me you are another with an alien brute strength. You have piqued me, offering to take control. And now with the shadow of the red cape, when my head is hanging low and my nostrils drip saliva on the sand, you are declaring yourself my master and asking me humbly to accept defeat. *Come,* you are saying, *I understand your passion, I will dispatch you quickly, like a lover . . .*

But *he is* the bull.

And who is to be dispatched, he or myself?

"Carmencita!"

"Yes little bull?"

"Nothing. Just Carmencita."

Communion. So?

I can love my murderer. I am certain of his intentions. I can trust him.

I slipped out from his arms before he became aware I was going.

"Carmencita!"

"I am going to bathe, darling. Will you bathe with me?"

"Of course!"

"Come then, put your hands on my hips and follow me in the dark. I know the way!"

We walked over the thick carpets to the door of my private bathroom. I turned on the light.

"Run the water," I said.

He bent down at once to the great black sunken bath and the water gushed in through the faucet.

We stepped in, one at either end, and locked our thighs. The water lapped up as far as my breasts, which floated on top like waterlillies.

"Passionate love is the fear of death, Prince! You want to sink out of existence under another's control."

He was stroking my left calf.

"You talk too much of death, Carmencita!"

"Our honeymoon ends in death, Prince."

"It is unbelievable!"

"It is certain."

He didn't reply.

"You'll break your word?"

"No."

"I shall be crucified, Prince, and tortured to death on the cross. I want death because I also fear it. To accept it in its most hideous form is to conquer it."

I smiled, pleased with myself.

"That is the contradiction of human existence, its negation is its affirmation and its affirmation is its negation."

"Let me kill you," he said quietly.

I stared at him.

"Would you, Prince? Would you!"

He paled.

I smiled.

"There is plenty of time, Prince. Soap my breasts and watch the bubbles break on my nipples!"

As he came over me with the soap it occurred to me that if I knew such a man were capable of killing me I might not find it necessary to leave him. Oh, foolish Prince . . .

ॐ

Later, while we were making love in the bath, coiling about under the warm and softened water, I whispered: "Will you really kill me, my darling?"

He replied only in body movements. He refused to answer. And then he came and his slime hung in the water like a strange sea creature, drifting like amoeba just under the surface where I laid my waiting mouth.

He watched fascinated and my eyes which held his were curtained with lust when the soft amorphous mass slipped in.

ॐ

Weeks of it until I slipped into a lethargy when lust made no response to his gentle caresses.

I tried hard to simulate it but he sensed that I was no longer with him and he became jealous and suspicious. He began to whine.

At that point I became cruel.

I told him that either he must whip me or I would whip him. I told him that he must obey or else I would break the pledge and leave at once. What did I care? I could walk out on both of them, on Miguel and himself, and return to the brothel where any night I could meet death by knife at the hands of a drunken sailor. Why not?

My Prince put on a soldierly air.

He would not raise a finger against me. He would accept to be whipped.

I made him hold the two posts of the big bedstead, thrust his rump slightly backwards and stand with his feet apart.

I selected a thin cane. This man could either die by my hand or he would consent to kill me What happened after that didn't matter. It would be interesting.

I looked professionally at his tightly packed buttocks, poor child that he was in reality!

I put my whole skill into the first stroke. He gasped with pain. I struck again aiming at the mark of the first. This time he flinched but obviously he had decided to prohibit himself from registering pain. Good enough. I would reduce him. My third stroke was perfect. In spite of himself his mouth burst open and he gasped. Terror was in his eyes at the fourth. I suppose he dimly realized that if I went on long enough I would kill him.

My fifth stroke was my second perfect one. It hurt him so much that he lifted one foot off the floor and, his hands losing their grip at the same time, he fell down on the floor beside the bed.

"Get up!" I hissed.

When he took his time, either pretending to be, or in fact, in great pain, I slashed him once beautifully across his naked belly and brought a minute curtain of blood sprinkling down.

He stared at it with a shocked expression in his eyes. His hand touched it and his fingers came away red.

"Do you still wish to be my lover?" I said.

"Yes!"

"And will you whip me or must I continue?"

He gritted his teeth.

"I will not whip you!"

"In that case, please be good enough to resume your former position; your hands on the bedposts."

He tried to unnerve me with a look but I gazed at him coldly, without pity.

I struck him six more times before he fell again in a heap, this time weeping freely and hiding his head in his arms. When he fell I struck him twice and after an interval of about five seconds a third time. Then I threw the cane at his bleeding body and left the room.

That night I passed alone, locked in another bedroom. Twice during the night he knocked at the door and implored me to let him in. "Go away," I said in a tired voice. "I may see you tomorrow if you obey me."

In the morning he waited for me outside the door.

"Carmencita!"

"You haven't slept?"

"Not a wink."

"So much the worse for you! We have a long day ahead of us. Immediately after breakfast I intend to whip or be whipped. I have a lust for thongs."

"Good God, how long must this go on!" the demented man cried.

"It is your own choice, Prince. You may leave the estate when you will. Or you may stay here and live your own life. But if you wish to have anything to do with me you must obey. You are much weaker than I, and I am no democrat! It is all very simple. Don't pretend you don't understand!"

"I believe you really mean to kill me!" he said with pretended awe.

"I should think it's quite obvious, Prince! Either you kill me or I kill you or we go our separate ways!"

"I don't believe you're serious, Carmencita!"

We were halfway through breakfast before I condescended to reply.

"Will you whip or be whipped?" I said, cold and sudden.

"I . . ."

Again he shot up this childish glance that was meant to unnerve me, the tragic hero glance, pretending he was powerless before fate.

"I take it that I flog you," I said brutally. "Good. It is leather today. It is quite different. You will soon be able to tell the difference blindfolded."

"Do you really mean you're going to flog me again!"

This was his last entreaty. His world was governed by certain conventions. He couldn't understand. Or didn't want to.

I spat in his face.

"Get out!" I said. "I will not see you today. I despise your cowardice. You are afraid of freedom. Then be like a good bull. I'll be your butcher."

With that I left him struck dumb in the parlor.

I avoided him for the rest of the day.

It took him three days to come round. Three wasted days!

"I'm ready for the leather," he said.

"Ah, I'm so glad, my darling!" I said huskily, slipping naked into his arms.

He kissed me desperately.

"Do you love me a little, Carmencita?"

"I adore you, my wonderful Prince!" I breathed. "Come, fuck me first! Show me you worship my cunt!"

Of course he came quickly. He was so afraid to come, for he was afraid of after.

Yes, there is always an after.

He was lying helpless, his emission quick and leaving him empty and unsatisfied.

I reached up to the wall and brought down the thongs.

"Oh, Carmencita!"

"Yes, my darling?"

"Could we not forget it, just for today?"

"Are you afraid?"

"No!"

"Then come! Today it will be easier for you. I am going to tie your hands and feet with thongs."

He got into position like a ghost. I bound him securely at his four extremities.

"But today I'm going to gag you," I said.

"No, Carmencita! Not that!"

"But why not? I will stop only when I feel like stopping anyway. I am taking my pleasure. Your noises distract me."

"I believe you're mad. Oh, Carmencita!"

"In that case, you had better leave the estate, sir. It is certainly not safe to be alone with a madwoman."

He fell silent.

I thrust a handkerchief in his mouth and tied it firmly in place with the silk belt of his dressing gown.

I took four thongs and began slowly.

This time his cock rose as he tried to enjoy the pain. I went round and sucked him off. He wriggled deliriously. But I was not finished. I beat him until he was unconscious. Then I cut him down, threw a rug over him, and took a walk about the grounds.

When I returned he had come to.

He was lying on the divan in his dressing gown, breathing heavily. I walked across to him and stroked his hair. Tears came to his eyes but he said nothing. I lay down beside him, brought my body close to his, and in that way we fell asleep.

That night we walked in the garden in the moonlight. He held my hand. I could feel that he was trying to say something but he did not seem to be able to speak. Perhaps he was not sure what it was he wanted to say or perhaps it was something he had said before and which I had already treated with scorn.

"Three days until the full moon," I said gazing up at the moon racing amongst cirrus clouds, little white wisps which seemed to be given off by the moon itself in traveling.

I sensed his desperation.

"It will be all over after the full moon," I said. "You will be well again and you will fall in love with some brilliant woman at court and you will marry."

"Never." He spoke quietly, without hope. I liked him.

"That's your affair," I said.

"And it means nothing to you?"

"Should it after I am dead?"

"There is no need for you to die."

"What about your word of honor."

"I would break it ten times over. But if you decide to live my word is not affected. I promised to do nothing to hinder you, nor to speak of it afterwards, but I didn't promise to drag you to the cross if you yourself chose against it. You would be safe, darling!" He took me in his arms and gazed down sadly into my eyes. "Miguel and his whole bloody crew would be at my mercy without you, for I am at your mercy and so at his. If you died I would no longer be at his mercy but he would be protected by my promise. If you choose to live he can touch neither you nor me and I can withold my protection. Did he tell you this? No? Ah, I see he didn't. Yes, Carmencita, upon you depends the future of the entire infamous Order. Yes, Count Miguel is making his last terrible bid to make it survive. He thinks that if he can marry his own reputation to that of the miracle, of the crucified virgin—there is a great deal of superstition in Spain—he will be strong enough to foil any official attempt to break up the Order. He may be correct. It would harden his own Cardinals, very powerful men, against the more Liberal elements who are trying to break it up. There has lately been dis-sension even amongst the Cardinals. Miguel's predecessor was a weak old man who had not the authority to stem the fear that arose in his own ranks from the rising public opinion. They have reason to fear. If they are exposed there will no doubt be some grave criminal proceedings against them. Seven Cardinals have already deserted and four of those have joined ranks with the Liberals." He stopped. "Oh, Carmencita, why not marry me? I can give you everything!"

"No, don't speak now. I want to know all about Miguel."

"Miguel found you—God knows where!—and held you in a state of readiness until just this moment when he was elected. He was expecting his predecessor to die for years. It's rumored he made four attempts on the old man's life. Even now it's nearly too late. But he thinks he can win by combining his election with the advent of the willing virgin." He smiled through his sadness and said with gentle irony: "That's you, Carmencita . . ."

"Yes."

"You must die on the cross or Miguel is finished. So you see he is not at all interested in your last passion nor in your virginity but only in the preservation of the Order in Spain.

"He had a great deal of luck with me. A number of years ago I was his worst political enemy.

"And suddenly I knew you weren't a virgin and the Order was in my power.

"But it is you who are the virgin. Don't you see, Carmencita? And you are his, married in body and soul. And that puts me in his power. I am powerless to strike him.

"And with you he both achieves his 'miracle' and silences an important Liberal.

"Sometimes I think he groomed you both for the cross and for me!"

"How?"

"There was no need to go so far with his publicity to make of his dedicated virgin victim a celebrated Queen of the *demimonde*. Public men are often foolish victims of such courtesans. And no one could compare with you. You would do anything, anything, you would die on the cross for passion, you could be vulgar and noble, chaste and licentious, pure and debauched. *No one would ever make love to you!* Miguel meant it. He is the most cunning devil in Spain. Even a genius."

"He is very clever," I said quietly.

We walked a little further in the garden. We kissed again. He kissed my breasts.

"Tell me, Prince, why . . ."

"Why do you call me 'Prince' ? You know my name."

"Because you don't want me to. Is it not obvious?"

"How cruel you are Carmencita!"

"Are you less cruel? Did you fall in love with me or did you want me for political reasons or is it the same thing in reality? But your personal reasons increased until you couldn't do without me. And so you try to change me and to mold me to your own pattern. If you succeed you too kill two birds with one stone, you win me and you destroy your most dangerous political enemy."

"How can you say so, Carmencita? How can you compare!"

I put my finger on his lips and sealed them.

"I want you to let me decide forever tomorrow morning, darling. If I decide against you, you must leave me at once and hold good to your promise to Miguel. If I decide against Miguel you can destroy him and create me."

"But I still have three days to influence you, Carmencita!"

"If I decide against you I need three days to prepare myself for the cross."

He was silent.

"Shall I have them? I am at your mercy, Prince. Will *you* be merciful?"

"Yes," he said quietly.

He took me in his arms. "Remember that I love you, my darling! It is of you I think always!"

"Then love me tonight!" I said, closing my eyes and turning my face up to his in the moonlight.

❧

The hands slipped deftly across my belly, the tongue sank deep in my cunt, the legs contained me, the belly straddled me; he made his best love that night.

But he made it for him, not for me, for there was neither thong nor knife in his hand as he offered love.

If he had offered that, if he had proven love, who knows, I might have changed my desires; what were those desires but the fruits of a disbelief in love? I am alone. The Prince is alone. Miguel is alone. The Prince lies. He tries to tell me that I am not alone. Miguel tells the truth. He tells me that I am.

Miguel, my love, be my executioner!